Totally Bound P..L.. .

**wind Warriors**
Tiger's Lily
Loco
Summer's Night

# TURBULENT RAIN

## CHEYENNE MEADOWS

Turbulent Rain
ISBN # 978-1-78430-307-5
©Copyright Cheyenne Meadows 2014
Cover Art by Posh Gosh ©Copyright October 2014
Interior text design by Claire Siemaszkiewicz
Totally Bound Publishing

# TURBULENT RAIN

# Dedication

For my parents, who continue to be my biggest fans.

# Chapter One

Slinking on her belly, Rain crept closer and closer to her target. Twigs poked into her sensitive stomach as the damp earth crusted on her clothing. Mud lodged under her short nails as she dug in for purchase on the slippery slope. All the while she was careful to be silent as she moved in upwind of her destination. A shiver coursed through her as a stiff breeze blew across her wet clothing. Steeling her resolve, she slid another few inches, not taking her eyes from the goal just another scoot or two ahead.

The new Spring Hill alpha pair would be officially taking the throne as mates any minute now. Rain dared not miss the historic event, though the participants belonged to a rival pack. Her curiosity and nosey nature demanded she watch the ceremony, even from a distance as an uninvited guest. Whispered rumors abounded about the individuals stepping up to the coveted position, and Rain couldn't wait to lay eyes on such famous and popular shifters. The fact her controlling alpha father would flip if she actually attended only sweetened the deal in her opinion, enough to convince her to take the risk.

A jagged rock tore into her inner thigh, sending a sharp sting straight to her brain. *This would be so much easier if I could just shift, damn it.*

Most wolf shifters could fully embrace their wolf side by the time they reached the age of eighteen. Much to her chagrin and her parents' dismay, she still hadn't been able to perform the big change. Not from lack of trying, either.

Stuck in human form, she stubbornly clung to her plan of seeing the alpha pair take their rightful place. Ignoring the discomfort, she nudged forward. Finally, she reached the pinnacle of the hill overlooking the ceremonial amphitheater of the Spring Hill Pack.

Dozens of people had gathered around. Some sat on rock benches. Others stood. A baby cried out, only to be shushed by his mother as she swaddled him and began to sway back and forth on her feet. An elderly silver-haired man stepped out onto the flattened stage area, looked over the crowd, then gestured to his right. A man with short dark hair walked out, tall and graceful. Black slacks covered his long legs, matching what appeared to be a black silk shirt, the fabric shimmering under the amphitheater lights. A smaller-framed woman followed, her waist-long black hair pulled into a thick braid, contrasting with the long white flowing dress that fluttered around her knees. She smiled at the man and intertwined her fingers with his.

That must've been the new pair. They made a handsome couple—young, attractive, and obviously happy. Yet, Rain didn't believe for an instant they were less than lethal if a situation called for downright brutality. The mark of a powerful leader.

Alphas achieved the top spot either through birthright or sheer aggressiveness. Just because one happened to be a child of an alpha pair didn't automatically give them the authority to rule or the ability to keep their alpha position throughout life. The title had to be earned, fought for, and held with command—another reason she would never hold the same position as her ancestors. She preferred to avoid bloodshed whenever possible, and the thought of watching her back at all times for a potential challenge to her rule didn't sit well. She wanted a life all her own, not one tied to the beck and call of a hundred others.

A smile crossed her face as she stared at the happy alphas, followed by a frown of confusion as another man stepped forward to take the female's free hand. He also dressed in solid black, his light blond hair stark against the darkness. Turning as a unit, they stood together before the old man.

*Not a pair. A threesome.* The fact only slightly surprised her, since some packs had accepted and embraced threesomes as ideal. However, never before had she heard of three people holding the title of pack alphas, a traditional position for a single alpha male and his alpha female mate. Maybe, just maybe, traditions were slowly changing in the Spring Hill Pack. If so, her family might follow suit. A blessing in her opinion—to leave the stingy, snobbish times behind and step into the present.

"Who the hell are you?"

Rain tensed and gasped as her heart sped. Swiveling around, she found a man staring at her, arms crossed over his chest as a severe frown marred his handsome face. A square chin promised stubbornness as black eyes sparked in the light. Jet black hair fell rakishly over his forehead, while longer locks tickled the collar of his matching shirt.

*The man has a flair for black. Big time.*

None of her senses alerted her to another's presence. Granted, she'd been distracted by the people below, but her advanced hearing and sense of smell should have detected an approaching person yards away, which meant this man excelled at stalking.

Slowly and carefully, she sat up then stood, making no quick movements that might set off the already snippy man. A wolf shifter if her nose proved correct. Just like herself. Only harder, sexier, and more than likely proficient with shifting.

Taking a moment to dust off her jeans, she watched his gaze wander down her body and back once more.

"I'm Rain." The whisper came across almost breathlessly as she took in his large build, firm muscles, and physical power. Intelligence showed in his eyes as did a bit of crankiness, judging by the downturned lips. While harsh, his expression didn't speak of cruelty or craziness. Instead, he appeared stern and unwavering.

"Rain. From where?" His baritone voice carried no farther than her ears and sent a thrill through her.

She might have been raised with wolf shifters who harbored a reputation for oozing sexiness just from a grin, chuckle, or from a confident strut, but this one took the cake. Sure, he frightened her to some degree with his obvious power and displeasure. He could snap her in half like a stick if he so desired. Yet, she'd never seen a man quite like him. Her heart pitter-pattered, breathing hitched, and her stomach knotted as she studied the most gorgeous man she'd had the pleasure to look upon in her young life.

"From around here." She waved her hand.

His eyes narrowed for an instant. Leaning in, he sniffed once, stepped decidedly into her personal space then sniffed once more, this time at her neck.

Rain held completely still, hardly daring to breathe. Everything about this man shouted dominant male and one not to be trifled with. If she resisted his inquisitive gesture, he'd only ensure she complied one way or another. Running would only prick his instincts to chase, ending with her most likely caught in a few quick bounds. Fisting her hands, she stoked her courage in order to avoid showing the fear washing through her in hard waves. He could tear out her throat from this distance, yet she banked on her first impression. He might be one grumpy bastard, but he wouldn't kill an innocent without sufficient cause. Spying on a mating ceremony hopefully didn't warrant such extreme punishment.

"Wolf shifter." He mumbled against her ear as he nuzzled the area for a greater scent. "Young." Another sniff. "And virginal."

*How embarrassing.* Thankful for the shadowy night, which hopefully covered her heating face, she swallowed around the lump in her throat. He must've had a talented nose in order to discover so many of her secrets so quickly. Her senses only told of his wolf shifter DNA. Nothing more. However, judging by his sheer yumminess, he'd left the label of innocent behind a while back. Women probably flocked to him now, only adding to his confidence, if not arrogance as well.

She opened her mouth then immediately shut it once more. No sense in trying to lie. If he could ascertain such information in less than thirty seconds, he could easily see through any falsehoods she might try to throw out.

Leaning back, he studied her face for a long moment. "Horizon Pack." He snarled as if the sound of the pack name brought forth disgust.

"I-I..." She stammered, not sure what to say. The fact the two packs didn't get along had been pretty much etched in stone for the past few centuries.

"You snuck in to watch the ceremony." He made the phrase a statement.

She shrugged. "Since I didn't receive an invitation, how else was I supposed to watch the big show?" Fear brought out her snarky side at times. Sarcasm became her frontline defense, which more often than not landed her in worse trouble because she pissed off the other person even more with her mouth.

His eyebrows furrowed as he absorbed her comment, even as his lips lifted to show a good bit of fang.

A tremor raced over her. She raised her chin and waited.

With a harsh curse, he grabbed her by the arm, leading her away from the spot she'd worked so hard to reach.

"Where are you taking me?"

He slowed his steps but didn't pause. "I'm escorting you to the edge of our pack lands. If you're smart, you'll run straight home and keep your damn mouth shut."

"Oh, believe me, the last thing I want to do is confess to my parents where I've been tonight. They'll make the princess in the tower story sound like a carnival ride, once they get a hold of me." She hurried along to keep pace. Her words replayed through her mind, causing her to stumble. *Idiot. Mentioning parents only brings about the next logical question.* If he found out she was a child of the alphas, who knows what he'd do.

Keep her for ransom. Send her back in a box. Tie her to the train tracks and wait for a train to come along.

He peered down at her. "Yeah, alpha parents aren't the most understanding about juvenile stupidity."

Her mouth fell open. "How...?"

He rolled his eyes. "How many female wolf shifters in this area are named Rain?"

She blew out a deep breath. Busted by her honesty.

They walked several more minutes before he spoke once more. "Why didn't you shift? You'd have been more difficult to see and track in your wolf form."

He already knew her standing in the pack, what was one more little secret among sort of friends? "I can't shift."

He stopped and stared down at her, still holding her upper arm in a gentle, yet firm grip. "What do you mean, you can't shift?"

Jet studied her. While petite, she had curves in all the right places. Athletic and youthful, she appeared more than capable of long distance runs across fields or meadows with energy to spare. A long, brunette ponytail swayed with each step, enticing him to run his fingers through the silky strands, to pull the lush richness close and inhale her unique scent. Again. The small sample he'd obtained earlier only whetted his interest and intrigued him. She reminded him of wildflowers, sweet with a little spice tossed in. The elixir proved intoxicating. His inner wolf sat up and took notice with a whimper of sudden need.

His body immediately followed, his groin tightening to the point of discomfort, solely from inhaling her delicious scent.

*What the hell?* Never before had he reacted so quickly. The realization rattled him, even as his instincts insisted they were right. *No way.*

Jet watched her nostrils flare as anger sparked in her alluring and unusual lavender eyes. "Just what I said. I can't shift."

The thought of her unable to perform the basic function of their species flabbergasted him. Her parents were alphas, a fact he'd easily pieced together once she confessed her name. The baby of the large family, she carried generations of powerful shifters in her blood. Surely she could change shapes if she just practiced a bit. While young, she was still more than old enough to achieve furry form.

"Have you tried?"

She blinked up at him. A myriad of emotions crossed her face ranging from indignation to anger to astonishment. "Of course I've tried. What do you take me for? A complete lackwit?"

His lips twitched at her short outburst. She had spirit and courage. He'd give her that. "Ah, so you're one of those late bloomers?"

She kicked at a loose pebble and lowered her head. "It seems so."

Shifting carried supreme importance in a pack. Those able to achieve their animal forms were popular, looked up to, respected, and even granted adult status within the group. Others who were unable to perform this rite of passage were considered still a child—no matter their real age—and often proved the butt of many jokes and cruel bullying. Self-esteem suffered, as did the person's spirit, receiving punishing blows that the individual might never quite recover from. Harsh words at such a sensitive time often were branded in their minds, a fact Jet could understand well.

Sympathy hit him square in the chest, a rarity for him. Such soft feelings were frowned upon by his pack, especially for wolves scaling the ladder of leadership. Adult males could show compassion and caring, although the tenderness was normally limited to mates and their young. For interlopers from another pack, niceness would be considered a potential downfall and unacceptable. Thus, he kept his mouth shut. No sense playing cheerleader for someone he'd be with for the next ten minutes, then probably would only see from afar for the rest of his existence.

His inner wolf growled and grew agitated at his thoughts. Surprised and a bit annoyed, he ignored the bellyaching grumbles in his head, focusing instead on scanning the area for danger or one of their own. If either of them were caught together, heads were bound to roll—whose depended upon which party stumbled across them first. Besides, she was too young. *In time*, he consoled his wolf. *All in good time.* He knew his wolf well enough not to question the sudden interest. All he had to do was sniff her again for a good reason to take hold.

"I get almost there then just can't do the final step," she said, as she began ambling forward once more. "I try. I really do. It's just not happening." Rain glanced up at him.

He sighed and called himself a thousand kinds of fool. Yet, he paused and met her gaze. "Shift. Do it now."

She blinked up at him. "Haven't you been listening? I can't."

"You're trying too hard. Just do it," he challenged.

She frowned, then closed her eyes and pursed her lips. "Fine. I'm trying. But don't be surprised when I say I told you so."

He reached out and placed one hand on the top of her head. A pleasant zing tingled through his fingertips as soon as he touched her. Arousal flared to a raging inferno a moment later. He grappled with his sudden rampant desire. Sucking in a deep breath, he focused back on the task at hand.

"Relax, stop talking and just listen." He waited for her shoulders to ease. Only then did he lower his voice and whisper in her ear, "Focus on your inner wolf. Hear her. Embrace her. Compel her forward. Do you have her?" His words came out raspy as he grappled with an almost undeniable urge to take what was his. Right here, right now.

"Yes."

The single word caressed his protective instincts, reinforcing something he could hardly believe. Someway, somehow, she belonged to him. Shoving his base needs and instincts to the side, he paid attention to the immediate issue, teaching the pretty little she-wolf to shift.

"Now picture yourself becoming the wolf. Let her free."

She stood as before with two legs and two arms, her face scrunched up in a grimace or avid concentration. Neither one appeared to be working.

"See!" Rain huffed and crossed her arms over her chest. Frustration and dejection flashed through her eyes.

"Let me guess...you're not known for your patience?" He shook his head but didn't remove his hand. Instead, he pulled her closer.

She balked. "What are you doing?"

"Teaching you to shift. Just trust me." He dropped his hands and waited.

After a long moment of silence, she grudgingly nodded. "Okay. Just no funny stuff."

He would have chuckled at her comment if his erection wasn't throbbing at the same time that his beast demanded he grab up Rain, throw her over his shoulder and carry her home to keep. Forever.

Instead, he wrapped her against his body in a tight hug. She remained stiff, yet she didn't struggle. Taking her actions as a positive, he circled her waist with one arm then cupped the back of her head with his free hand. Leaning in, he sniffed her neck once more, savoring the unique scent that jacked up his want all the more. Her presence didn't just cause him to be horny. She also fired his natural inclinations toward a mate—protection, caring, and lending a helping hand when needed.

He nuzzled her cheek and licked her earlobe. "You're so tight. It's a wonder you can breathe. Just relax, Rain. Relax and let me lead."

Slowly, by inches, her muscles eased. Only when she melted into his larger frame did he speak again as he placed small kisses along her jawline. "Find your inner wolf. Talk to her. Coax her. Feel her." He trailed the tip of his tongue over her collarbone before beginning a journey up the column of her slender throat. "Got her?"

"Yes." She nearly purred the word.

He settled his lips over hers for a second, enough to taste her unique flavor and commit it to memory.

He heard her sharp intake of breath and knew she felt the same electricity between them as he did. Her hands worked their way to circle his neck as she lifted on tiptoe to lessen the space between them. "What now?"

"You have to believe in yourself. Know you can and will do this. Embrace your inner beast." He meshed their lips once more, added enough spice and lazy aggressiveness to the kiss that Rain opened her mouth on a gasp. Seizing the opportunity, he delved in, seeking her depths after a quick game of tag with her tongue.

She moaned and edged closer, rubbing her body against his.

Easing back, Jet grinned at the definite smell of arousal coming from Rain. *Oh, yeah.* She definitely felt the budding passion between them.

Before they could get too carried away, he loosened his hold, separating from her tender lips just enough to speak. "You and your wolf ready?"

She blinked up at him as if slightly dazed. Slowly, she bobbed her head. "I think so."

"Know so."

She exhaled. "We're ready."

Jet watched her face and focused. "Now shift." He used his hand on the back of her head to gently nudge her in the right direction.

Nothing happened for a long moment then slowly her body began to change. Bones crackled and crunched, and she morphed from human to animal. In the next moment, he stared at a nearly solid white wolf, small, even for a female. Those lavender eyes remained the same, only widened in pure astonishment then with unbridled excitement. She jumped and bounced, her joy abundant and contagious.

He grinned proudly. "See? Not so hard after all."

Her muzzle widened into a smile, complete with pink tongue hanging out as she panted.

Jet squatted down, spread her shirt out on the ground, placing the rest of her clothes, shoes included, in the middle, then used the sleeves to tie the bundle into a nice little package. She might be able to compose her own clothes as most shifters could magically do, but if she returned in something other than what she wore when she left, her family might notice. Best for her to change back rather than chance them discovering she'd snuck out.

"Don't forget these." He held out the parcel to her, patting her head when she gingerly took the object. "And change back before you arrive home. You don't want anyone to figure out where you've been."

She wagged her tail and dropped her pack for a moment. After licking his hand, she picked up the garments once more with her sharp teeth and sped toward home.

Jet stood, his heart clenching at the sweet show of gratitude as he watched her zip across the rough terrain that led toward her pack lands. He smiled as a feeling of rightness cascaded over him. Something told him he and Rain would meet again soon enough. Only the next time, he'd do more than teach her to shift. A whole lot more.

"Run while you can, little Rain. Because one day, I'll catch that cute tail of yours and make you my own."

With one more glance, he turned on his heel and sauntered back the way he'd come.

# Chapter Two

*Five years later*

"Thank you for shopping with us. Please come again soon." Rain handed the plastic bag to the salt-and-pepper-haired lady and waved as she headed toward the door, clutching her recent purchases.

"We're going through material like mad today. Think we'll need to put in an extra order?" Autumn asked, as she leaned back against the long cabinet used to first cut material, then fold. Her shoulder-length chestnut hair hung loose today. The dark green slacks and matching blouse complemented her coloring, bringing out the hint of red in her locks.

Rain turned her attention from the door to her employee. After opening the doors of Fabrics and More four years ago, Rain had quickly decided she needed to hire a helper when business had begun to pick up then shoot through the roof as word had spread of her little store specializing in fabrics, yarn, and needlework items. Autumn had immediately applied. They'd hit it off.

"Maybe. We'll check inventory at the end of the day. If we're low, I'll call the wholesaler and see if they can do another run this week."

"I'll go do the count now before another wave of customers hits." Autumn grabbed a note pad and pen then dashed off toward the back of the small room.

Rain shook her head with a grin. Hiring Autumn had been the best decision she'd ever made, even if the other woman's energy left her in the dust. Autumn zipped here and there, reminding Rain of a Jack Russell terrier, never seeming to tire throughout the entire day. No wonder she maintained a slim and trim figure.

Her phone rang. Picking it up, she glanced at the caller ID, frowned, and immediately answered. "Hello?"

"Rain. How are you, dear?" Her mother's voice came across strong, just like the woman herself. She held the alpha female position for a reason. Logical, compassionate, and normally easygoing, she could turn into a fierce predator at the drop of a hat—a perfect complement to Rain's sterner father.

"I'm fine. Busy at work, as usual."

"That's wonderful. Your father and I had reservations about your moving away from the pack to live amongst humans, but it sounds like you're doing quite well."

The business had been a major success. She'd scrimped and saved for years, finally taking a gamble on her lifelong dream. Still, she didn't get crazy with the profits, instead maintaining a steady course of frugal living until she felt completely confident the store would withstand any downturn in the economy. That was why she still lived in the apartment above the store, paying one rent instead of two if she'd decided to set up house elsewhere.

"I am. Really."

"Glad to hear it. Now, what I'm calling about. This Saturday is the yearly congregation for the pack. Your father and I expect you to attend."

"But I'm working. Saturday is our busiest day, you know." She stood firm. No way was she willingly returning to the pack for a huge meet and greet.

"Rain Serena Winters. You're a member of this pack, daughter of the ruling alphas. It's your duty to attend this function." Her mother's sweet voice turned firm and commanding.

Rain's shoulders dropped as she puffed out a breath. She'd known that the annual event fast approached but had hoped to be excused from the event due to her work. No such luck.

"I'll ask Autumn to work."

The last thing she wanted to do was pack up and drive an hour to the pack lands, spend the weekend ducking pack males who wanted nothing more than to claim her, while her parents watched over her as if she was a small child on her first outing. The persistent pack males bore much of the responsibility for her deciding to open her store fifty miles away. Since she'd reached adolescence, wolf shifter men had followed her around, asking—and some nearly insisting—she accept their offer for first a fling, then possible matehood. None of them caught her interest—not even the smallest heart throb or drool. Besides, she questioned whether any truly wanted her for herself. Because of her birthright, they would have a step up in status if they mated a daughter of the alpha. While she couldn't change her parents or genetics, she could decide on her own mate, and

Horizon Pack had nothing to offer her in that department.

"That's better. We'll expect you on Saturday morning. That'll leave plenty of time for us to chat with you before the festivities begin."

Biting back a groan, Rain gathered her composure. She already knew what they wanted to lecture her about. Finding a mate. They had the same lengthy and painful discussion every time she visited. Same argument, different day, and they always came to the same impasse. "Fine. I'll be there early."

"Wonderful. I'll tell your father and siblings you'll be here by nine."

"Bye, Mother." Rain clicked off the phone and slipped it in her pocket with a deep sigh of resignation.

"Let me guess. Your parents want you to come home again."

"Yep. This weekend is the annual family reunion. I'm expected to attend." Since Autumn was human and unaware of shifter existence, Rain didn't elaborate further, despite the feisty brunette being her best friend.

Autumn grinned as she walked up to the counter. "By the look on your face, I can tell they're playing matchmaker and clamoring for grandchildren."

Rain nodded. "As always." She slouched in defeat.

"You know how to change that, don't you?"

"Join an expedition to the North Pole?"

Autumn chuckled. "Nope. Find your own man. That'll get you off the hook with them."

*If only it were that easy.* Rain frowned at her friend. "I'm not sure I want one. They're way too much trouble."

After tearing off the slip of paper, Autumn stuck the bright yellow note to the table in front of Rain. "Oh, I don't know. I suppose if you find the right one, they might be worth all the effort."

"You've been reading romance novels again?"

With a bright laugh, her employee headed across the store. "I'll gladly work Saturday, Rain. Go play with your family for a weekend. You never know. You just might find the man of your dreams waiting."

"Uh huh." She plucked the note from the desk, glanced at the numbers and picked up the phone. "Like a snowball's chance in hell."

\* \* \* \*

"Rain? Are you listening?"

Her father's low voice brought her attention back to the uncomfortable conversation at hand. As soon as she'd arrived, her parents had corralled her and had begun talking on the subject that made her cringe each and every time. Ignoring their babble proved one way to survive the polite tongue-lashing fairly unscathed — until they caught her and insisted upon her full attention.

"Yes, I'm listening." Her tone reflected the boredom she felt. Shifting in the hard wooden chair at the kitchen table, she folded her hands and prayed for patience.

"We're just concerned, sweetheart. You're twenty-three years old. Most other pack females of your age have long since been mated and had pups. All your sisters have as well. They're happy, too." Her mother droned on.

"I'm not unhappy where I'm at, Mom." Rain set her back teeth, resigned to enduring the lecture once more. Not as if she hadn't had practice. They'd said the same words to her for the past few years, ever since she reached the age of adulthood. She barely resisted the urge to roll her eyes.

"It's just unnatural for a female wolf shifter to not be mated. There's an abundance of qualified and decent males. Just pick one." Her father's gray gaze bore into her own.

"That's the problem, Dad. I don't just want to 'pick one' like I would pick a pair of shoes. I need more out of the relationship. I need love." There. The truth came out. Not that her determined parents would be swayed by such a fickle emotion, but it was the absolute truth. She couldn't envision gluing herself to a man just because that's what females did. She needed more — so much more.

Her parents shared a long look then her mother sighed dramatically. "How are you going to find love when you live among the humans, well away from pack lands? Isolation doesn't lead to interaction with eligible men."

"That's why you're going to stay the whole weekend and socialize — not just with family, but meet the full pack."

"But …!"

"No buts, Rain. The pack has changed in the past few years. There are men who have matured into adulthood, even a few new members. You'll meet each and every one." His stern expression showed that he meant serious business. "Your wolf will know when she meets her mate, so forget this romantic notion of love. You'll choose a mate before the weekend is over."

A flicker of fear resounded through her gut. "I'll agree to meet the men, but I won't promise to choose this weekend." She lifted her chin, refusing to be cowed by his order.

"You *will* choose this weekend, young lady. We've given you enough time already. It's well past time you find a mate to care for you. Watch over you. Settle you down to your proper place in the pack."

She bristled at her father's ancient beliefs, so contrary to her own. This was the very reason she'd chosen to move away, to live her own life, to experience independence and freedom, to really be herself, not just another broodmare for her growing wolf pack.

"Or?"

"Or I'll choose for you."

Astonishment and horror sent a shudder through her body even as her mouth gaped open. "You wouldn't!"

"I can, and I will."

"Rain, dear. We're just looking after your best interests, giving you the option to pick the one you want." Her mother reached over the table and patted her hand.

"I'm only twenty-three, not one hundred and eighty-seven!"

"As we said before, almost all females are already mated by the time they hit twenty-one for their own safety and comfort. We've been lenient with you far too long. Since you don't seem to be moving toward finding a mate yourself, we made the decision to step in." Her mother's voice hardened as she studied her for a long moment. "Mate or not, your heat cycles will begin, if they haven't already. Your body will drive you to find a mate. Better now when you can make a rational decision than later, when hormones might influence a poor choice."

Her father broke in, "Not to mention an unmated female in heat only begs trouble among the unmated males. Fights break out, leading to distraction. The female herself is at risk from overly aggressive males determined to claim the female for their own. All this nonsense can be avoided if the female just finds her man."

Rain understood their reasoning — to a certain extent. Wolf shifter females typically went into their first heat when they reached adulthood and kept on a fairly consistent schedule for life. Those who bucked tradition soon discovered their bodies wouldn't be denied or deterred by such a trivial issue of not presently having a mate by her side. They suffered the maddening event of heat anyway, the body's innate way of driving the females wild with lust until they matched up with a man out of sheer necessity and need. Thus, two singles would mesh into a mated couple.

Unless, they found their true mate. Immediately upon becoming sexually active with a true mate, a female is sent right into heat, no matter where she happened to be in her cycle — her body's way of differentiating a true mate from a chosen mate.

She knew all this from personal experience. The tide of overwhelming desire had washed over her once before, demanding an outlet. Stubbornness and determination had helped her through it and would do so again. She ruled her body, not the other way around.

"Time has come for you to take a mate, Rain. We're going to make sure you do so," her father warned. "Don't make me pass judgment for your willful defiance."

Tears threatened, but Rain blinked them back. Wolves saw emotional outbursts as weak, and weakness had no place in the pack. Anger boiled in her belly, but she bit back a sharp retort, remembering her place. Despite being her parents, the couple sitting across the table also happened to be her pack alphas. Disobedience and insubordination wouldn't be tolerated, no matter the relationship ties. Pack laws and survival depended on everyone toeing the line and following orders. Those who refused faced ostracism or, in worst case scenarios, a brutal death. Her parents would never resort to such extremes with her. However, shunning her would be a definite possibility. As much as she liked living away from the pack, that didn't mean she truly desired to be cut off from her family, never seeing or speaking to them again. Her heart clenched at the thought.

Straightening her spine, she glared at her imposing father, watching his face carefully for an indication that he intended to follow through on his threat. "You will accept whomever I choose?" She spoke softly and clearly, needing this point well ironed out, her only true caveat of control left.

"As long as he's an adult wolf shifter, I'll accept your choice." His words held truth and hard promise. Absolutely no sign of wavering crossed his face. As much as she'd love to call his bluff, he certainly didn't appear to be willing to give an inch on this matter.

"No questions asked?" She pressed for complete clarity.

Her parents nodded. "No questions asked," her mother answered for them both.

"Fine." She lifted her chin and glared at them both. "If you'll excuse me, I need to get some fresh air." Without waiting for a proper dismissal, she walked out of the door before she said something she'd regret later.

A tumult of emotions rode Rain hard, anger leading the way. How dare her parents—who supposedly loved her unconditionally—order her to choose a man in the next forty-eight hours to spend the rest of her nine hundred plus years with! Didn't they understand love didn't happen with such limits? While she believed in love at first sight, that didn't mean she expected such a luxury and an easy solution to slap her in the face at the festivities later today. Yet, at the same time, how could she introduce herself, shake a man's hand, and determine him the man for her? Obviously, her parents had lost their minds.

She saw no way out of her present mess. Sure, she could pack up and leave, head home at once. Good in theory, poor in long-term solution. Her father would send someone to collect and bring her back then place her under house arrest until she fulfilled his command. She could simply refuse and confess on Sunday afternoon that none of the men caught her eye. Sure, and chance her father dropping the hammer on his threat, picking out a mate for her. As much as she hated the idea, she believed he'd follow through under the heading of caring for his youngest daughter.

Her parents probably thought they were doing her a favor, ensuring her protection and happiness by placing a man at her side. While that might've worked for other females, Rain tended to buck traditional ideas of female behavior, wants, and needs—always had, always would. Few females saw an independent life for themselves, instead focusing their energy on finding a high ranking man to provide completely for their needs. They worked hard to primp and flirt, catching the eyes of the man they wanted, and hoping he'd offer to tie the knot. Housekeeping and children became their goal. Old fashioned ideals that made Rain cringe with distaste.

As much as she hated the idea of being forced into such a constrictive mold, she still couldn't find an escape clause. For all intents and purposes, she was trapped. Find a mate in two days or suffer one of her parents' choosing.

Frustration and a caged feeling built up, nearly choking her with rage. She had to get away from there, at least for a while—clear her head and find some way out of this nightmare.

After storming to her car, she quickly shucked her clothes, using the big SUV for cover. She gathered up her garments, shoes included, then dropped them onto the rear, driver's-side floorboard. She slammed the door shut, then immediately shifted into her wolf form, spun around, and sprinted toward the east, barely paying attention to where she went as hot tears swam in her eyes.

# Chapter Three

"Damn."

Jet grinned wickedly as he towel-dried his hair, his eyes landing on Garrett, his mate. They'd met at an inter-pack meeting, hit things off hard and fast then decided to take the leap to matehood. Time had flown by with days full of teasing and bantering while their nights were filled with blazing hot sex. Always before, Jet grew bored with lovers—not Garrett. No matter how many times they came together in passion, each event only whetted his hunger for more.

Standing a couple inches shorter, Garrett sported charcoal-colored eyes, which complimented his sandy blond, thick, collar-length hair. His muscles bunched and extended with every movement of his sturdy frame, the mass a gorgeous complement to the passion oozing from the man's very pores. Quick to grin and laugh, Garrett provided a softer side to Jet's own more temperamental nature. Garrett held his own position within the pack as a high ranking beta. He worked hard in the security division along with Jet, and proved quite popular with the entire population. His easygoing nature won him tons of friends, even those who normally gave Jet a wide path. A fact he teased Jet about often.

Garrett's gaze raked Jet's body up and down before finally settling on the groin area. "After this morning, I wouldn't have thought you could get hard again so soon."

Jet shrugged. He would have agreed after three pounding sessions of non-stop sex before they fell apart from exhaustion. Normally, he'd have his fill for a couple of days. With Garrett, he never had enough.

"Seems you're quite an inspiration." He glanced at the prominent bulge in his mate's jeans and licked his lips.

Garrett shook his head. "Uh huh." After stepping forward, he fell to his knees, wrapped his fingers around Jet's erection, and ran the tip of his tongue across the tip. "Mmmm. Tasty as ever."

Jet sucked in a breath and let the towel fall from his fingers. That one little caress threw gasoline on his rampant arousal and drew a low groan of need from his throat. His cock jerked in a desperate plea for more.

"We've got guard duty in fifteen minutes." He gritted the words out as Garrett opened wide and drew Jet's aching manhood deep inside his mouth, then commenced licking. "Shit, that feels good. So good. You're the best ever at giving head."

"Mmmmm." Garrett moaned, the vibrations strumming Jet's dick into heightened glory. Rocking back, his mate released his prize. "And you've got the largest dick I've ever seen. Absolutely gorgeous."

Jet's head fell back as the words stroked his libido all the more. His endowment left most men in the dust, even amongst wolf shifters who cornered the market on huge cocks. Grateful for the generous gift, he'd found not all sex partners appreciated his immense size. Some women had simply walked out after seeing him naked. More than a few men had blinked, cussed then backed away, claiming to want no part of him. None of that mattered now. Garrett not only enjoyed his dick, he reveled in it, begging for more every chance he had. Jet fisted his hand in his mate's hair and pulled him forward at the same time thrusting his hips until he was lodged deep in Garrett's mouth. For a couple of minutes, he guided his lover's motions before finally gritting his teeth and stepping back.

"Strip. Now."

Garrett's deep gray eyes met his own as a wide grin appeared on his face. "Eager much?"

Jet snorted. "We're short on time. I figured you'd rather come than run the perimeter with a full blown hard-on."

"Yeah. Good thinking." Garrett's hands flew over his clothes, leaving him nude in a matter of seconds.

The sight only added to Jet's heightened excitement. Garrett's body, from the tip of his blond head to the strong shoulders, wide chest, six pack abs, and down to his powerful legs made heads turn. Add in a muscular ass to grip his cock in all the right ways and a glorious erection made for licking, and Garrett rated at the top for downright handsomeness. Combined with a happy-go-lucky personality and teasing grin, he made the fabled Adonis pale in comparison.

"I can't get enough of you." The whispered words carried easily in the silent room.

"Ditto." Garrett reached out to wrap his fingers around Jet's cock once more. He measured the length with a snug grip.

At the end of his control, Jet sucked in a calming breath. "On the floor."

Garrett raised an eyebrow but quickly followed orders, lying down and rolled to his side. Jet followed suit, sliding down on his opposite side to face his mate, with his head to Garrett's feet. Without preamble, he grasped Garrett's erection, adjusted his position then flicked his tongue over the swollen head.

"Yessss." Garrett moaned low in his chest, trembled, then fastened his mouth over Jet's jutting shaft, his tongue and lips swirling, caressing, pushing Jet to pinnacle.

Hurrying to catch his partner up, Jet focused hard on pulling Garrett's rod deep inside his mouth, swallowing when he felt the tip brush his throat. He groaned deeply, letting the vibrations roll over his lover's sensitive cock. With enthusiasm, he lashed his tongue around the rigid pole, sucked in hard, and ever so lightly ran his fangs up and down the length as he bobbed his head back and forth. Jet delved between Garrett's legs, found his low hanging balls, and gently weighed them before gingerly giving them a tug.

Garrett's body tightened like a bowstring.

With one more pull, Jet took Garrett deep, feeling the tingling begin in his own balls.

A hard lapping tongue circled Jet's tip sending him straight into orbit. He cried out around Garrett's cock, his back arched, as wave after wave of ecstasy overcame him. A moment later he began to swallow as Garrett reached his peak. An endless stream of semen shot into the back of his mouth, the salty taste a sip of ambrosia.

Garrett twitched once more then winced when Jet ran his rough tongue over the slit, cleaning up each and every drop.

By the time Jet had finished, Garrett had done the same for him, leaving him sated and sensitive. Rolling to his back, Jet met Garrett's gaze with a lop-sided grin. "You can do that anytime you want."

Garrett matched his smile.

"Except now. We've got perimeter duty and if we're late, I'm pretty sure my brother will kick both our asses." Hunter, Jet's oldest brother and pack supreme alpha, never let anyone slide, especially his brothers — no matter the excuse.

"Too bad. I was going to suck you hard again, then bend over the couch..."

Jet jumped to all fours, turned around, and sealed his lips over Garrett's. After a long, thorough taste, he sat back on his heels. "Later, mate. After work." Upon slapping his partner on the ass, Jet stood and headed toward the bedroom to dress.

"Promise?" Garrett called from the living room.

"Oh, yeah. I'll be balls deep in your ass before supper. That's a promise." After digging out clothes, he dressed with a wry grin on his face. Life with Garrett couldn't be better.

* * * *

Jet grinned in happy remembrance. They presently patrolled the lush, flat meadow where he and Rain had reconnected a couple of days after he'd taught her to shift. Since the area lined the border between their pack lands, both groups used the space now and again, especially young lovers searching for a bit of privacy and freedom from prying eyes. He'd been doing much the same thing then as he did now, checking things out, when Rain had dashed over, enticed him into a quick game of tag, and they'd spent a few minutes running free as a spirited pair.

He'd enjoyed that short time immensely and missed her to this day. Unfortunately, last he'd heard, she'd decided to live her life with the humans a good distance away.

Perhaps he needed to pay her a friendly visit.

"I don't see anything that we haven't seen a hundred times before." Garrett sighed and moved closer to Jet, nudging him in the ribs. "Bet you can't catch me." With a wry grin, he shucked his clothes at a frantic pace then shifted into his wolf form.

"You're asking for it." Jet stood naked for only a fraction of a second before transitioning into his coal black furry form, glorifying in the ability to morph into a powerful predatory beast.

With a yip of excitement, Garrett spun around and sprinted off, Jet hot on his heels.

Jet couldn't help but grin at his mate's happy and contagious antics. Garrett reminded him how to let loose and enjoy life. Just one of the many reasons he loved him and they meshed so well.

They sped over the terrain. Each time he pulled in close enough to pounce, Garrett ducked to the left, forcing Jet to circle around and pour on another burst of speed to catch up once more. Panting from the exertion, Jet reveled in the game, knowing as soon as they returned home, Garrett would submit readily, more than eager to pursue a different form of play.

They'd been instantly drawn to one another the day they'd met, couldn't keep their hands off each other, and set a furious pace to accepting a bond of matehood. He'd never regretted a single day with Garrett, could never see a reason why he would. They were just too well matched to have any major issues.

Jet loved being with Garrett, and no other person made him feel as loved, special, or sexy as him—probably never would.

Garrett and he had spoken about women several times in their three years together. Each leaned more toward men but had had their fair share of women as well. They were comfortable with their bisexuality and often pointed out sexy people to each other, even absently tossed out possibilities of taking another to their bed. A threesome had never panned out, and they'd pretty much dropped the topic.

Threesome matings had become more and more common, almost equaling traditional couples in numbers overall. A few packs still stuck by the old ways—frowned on male-male couples or those that involved more than a single male and a single female. Luckily, those groups were slowly evolving or dying out as more open-minded members chose to quit the pack in favor of either being on their own or trying to situate themselves into more freethinking groups.

The Spring Hill pack to which Jet belonged held quite liberal ideas on the subject of matings. They had an open arms policy to any pairing, no matter the gender or number. Garrett's Golden Branch Pack sat somewhere in the middle. Same sex couples and threesomes weren't encouraged but, at the same time, weren't rejected or bullied. Jet liked to think living with Spring Hill had liberated Garrett's thoughts on the matter and allowed him to open up as a free and confident man who just happened to be mated to another man—Jet.

After zipping through a meadow, Garrett traveled along the forest's edge, skillfully navigating a bit of uneven terrain dotted with downed trees. With a lurch, he headed toward a grassy patch, Jet in hot pursuit. Just as Jet prepared to leap, Garrett slammed on the brakes and reversed course.

*Damn, he's quick.* Jet mentally kicked himself for falling for Garrett's crafty tricks. With more determination, he circled back around and took dead aim at corralling his mate this time.

The scent of another wolf wafted in the air. Before he could do more than slow down, a small, white canine pounced, knocking hard into him, sending them both rolling and tumbling until they slid to a stop in a small heap.

Jet inhaled deeply, his nose buried in the thick fur of the smaller wolf's neck. Memories sprang to life as he recognized the unique scent. Sensual longing hit him hard just like the last time they met. His cock leaped to attention as he wagged his tail in excited welcome. Only one woman had that effect on him. Rain.

Belatedly, he heard a low growl, glanced to the side and found Garrett poised for attack on the still-prone Rain, his lips pulled back to expose long, deadly fangs. Protective instincts kicked in immediately. After gaining his feet, he planted himself between the two, effectively stopping his mate from coming one step closer to the female.

Garrett stared at him in shock for a long moment then tilted his head in bewilderment. Unable to explain covered in fur, Jet quickly morphed into his human form, instantly covering himself with clothing in the process with a quick, magical thought. He couldn't hide the bulge in the front of his jeans or the scent of his arousal but didn't honestly care.

"Rain?"

The smaller wolf peeked up at him first in confusion then her eyes sparked in recognition. She shifted forms, only sat naked for an extra couple of seconds before material covered her female figure.

"Jet?"

Those lavender eyes bored into his soul. His heart clenched as he stared at the woman he hadn't seen in years, although it seemed like yesterday. She hadn't changed much, simply had grown more beautiful, more alluring. Long brunette hair cascaded down her back, drawing attention to her feminine curves. Her oval face carried little makeup, but she didn't need any. Natural beauty radiated from her. The brief glimpse of her nakedness set his mouth to watering and burned into his brain ready for use in future wet dreams.

His inner beast whimpered and whined, refusing to leave her again. He concurred, thrilled to run into her once more, especially in the same area they'd ran together once before, so long ago.

Jet couldn't wipe the grin off his face.

He glanced over, found Garrett back to human form and dressed, standing close by. Satisfied the threat had dissipated, he appraised Rain once more.

"Still having a bit of trouble with your magic, huh?" Jet teased.

She shrugged, sniffed, and wiped at her eyes. "Always. Some of us aren't as adept as others."

Jet shook his head. "Some of us are impatient and easily distracted, too."

Rain rolled her eyes. "Spoken like a true alpha. Know-it-all."

"Uh huh. We have a few redeeming qualities, you know."

She snorted and twisted to eye Garrett. "Who's your new friend?"

Jet quickly did the introductions, still amazed Rain stood before him. "Rain, Garrett. Garrett, Rain."

She shot Garrett a tentative smile. "Hi."

"Hello," he answered quietly, curiosity written clearly on his face.

"Back to visit or to stay this time?" Jet hoped for the latter, unwilling to let her get away again. The first time, she'd been too young. Today, age wouldn't stop him from claiming her for his own.

Rain's face pinched into a severe frown before she glanced at the earth beneath her feet. "I'm not sure."

Catching the tension in her voice, he sensed her genuine upset. He raked Rain with a long stare, concerned. "What's wrong?"

"Nothing." Her voice broke.

Jet stepped forward until she held out a hand, stopping him in his tracks. He shared a look with Garrett, noting that his mate had picked up on the same signs as he had, judging by his tense jaw and frown.

"Really, it's…nothing." She backed up a couple of steps, although her gaze remained locked on him.

"Rain. It's something. Tell me." His voice lowered to a coax dripping with honey.

Her head fell back for a second. She sucked in a breath, then stared at them both. "My father ordered me to find a mate this weekend. No excuses."

"How can he do that? He's just your father. No one can force you to accept a man." Garrett tilted his head.

Breath whooshed out of Jet, only to be replaced by livid fury. How dare her father back her into such a corner? Break her heart and put her at such potential risk? "He can if he's the supreme alpha of the pack," Jet explained quietly, checking his anger for the moment, though he fisted his hands in an effort to maintain control.

Garrett's eyebrows shot up. "Which pack?"

"Horizon," Rain answered on a whisper.

"Damn." The beta shook his head.

Horizon fell into the category of absolutely uptight and resistant to change. Compared to Spring Hill, Horizon lived in the Dark Ages.

Kicking his mind into gear, Jet frantically searched for a way out. He had to protect Rain, his instincts and inner wolf demanded nothing less. She was meant for him, damn it, not for some lackey appointed by her interfering father. *There has to be a way around this. Just how?* An idea began to form in his head.

"He's letting you pick, right?"

Rain nodded. "He just said an adult male wolf shifter. That's all his requirements. I made him promise no questions asked."

A pregnant silence followed.

The answer shone like a lighthouse beacon on a stormy night. Jet met Rain's gaze and spoke words straight from his heart. "Choose me."

Garrett's mouth dropped open. Guilt settled over his shoulders as he realized he'd left his mate out in the cold without the decency of consulting with him first. He couldn't help it. He'd found the perfect solution to Rain's dilemma. He'd always known they belonged together. So, the timing stunk. Some things couldn't be helped.

She stared at Jet for a long moment, obviously considering his offer. Hope sparked in her eyes. "My father would be furious if I chose someone outside the pack, particularly an alpha from Spring Hill." Her frown slowly eased into a soft smile. "It would be a fitting revenge for his heavy handedness and ridiculous demands." Then her face fell. "But I couldn't ask that of you. It's a mating, a long term commitment. I can't stick you with centuries of misery because of your knight in shining armor chivalry."

"I want to do this."

"No. It's not fair. I'll just find another way out of this mess." Her tone fell flat. "I'm not trapping you this way."

He sidled closer. "You said yourself your options consist of choosing one for yourself, having him one choose for you, or leaving your family forever. There's not a lot of wiggle room in that." He stared at her, curious for the reason of her continued resistance. "Did you have a man in mind already?"

She shook her head, looked up then turned her gaze on Garrett. "No. I didn't want to consider being tied down as a mate this early in life. I need space and independence, to be my own person instead of a broodmare for the pack." Rain blew out a breath. "I thought I had another hundred years before being forced into such a decision."

Just because her pack expected each female to mate early in life didn't mean she had the same goals. Women could be independent, several women in his pack proved that very fact. Plenty of time in a thousand year lifespan to find a mate, settle down, and start a family.

"At least you have me. Us. Garrett and I." Jet glanced back at Garrett, noticed the building storm on his face. He'd make it right. Later. After he got Rain all settled. He reached out and cupped Rain's cheek. "We'll stand with you. Get through this weekend. Then we'll figure out where to go from there."

"Are you sure?" Her gaze locked on Jet.

"I'm sure." He pecked her forehead and smiled. "Besides, a Spring Hill member getting the goat of the Horizon lead alpha will be the stuff of legend. My pack will chuckle about that for generations to come." He worked to lighten the mood and put a smile back on her pretty face. She deserved happiness, not sadness and a life full of regrets all due to her father's crazy meddling.

Garrett growled low in his throat. "You're going through with this insane plan? Mating the daughter of the Horizon alpha for a practical joke? Have you lost your ever-loving mind?"

Jet turned to him. "Why not? Rain has to pick someone. I'd rather she pick us than some stupid idiot from her own pack who might treat her poorly. It'll benefit us both. What's wrong with that?"

"What's wrong with that?" Garrett's voice rose as he threw up his arms in exasperation. "We're mated — or did you conveniently forget? You're offering matehood to someone I just met literally one minute ago. Don't I have a say in this?"

Rain flinched but remained mute.

"We're mates, and I love you. You know that." Jet sighed and ran a hand through his hair. He understood Garrett's rage and disbelief, but he couldn't explain things here and now, not in front of Rain. Once they were alone, he'd talk until the cows came home in order to make Garrett understand why she was so important to him, why he couldn't leave her to her own devices in this mess. "We'll discuss this later." He bobbed his head and stared at Garrett for a long moment before turning his attention back to Rain. "When do you want to present us to your father?"

"Tomorrow at noon would be good." She peeked sheepishly at Garrett. "I know this is unprecedented and probably unwelcomed, but I really am desperate. If I don't choose a man this weekend, my father will choose one for me. Refusal will result in ostracism from the pack. They're my only family." She stepped forward and lightly ran her fingers across Garrett's hand. "Please. Just think about it." Pivoting, she focused on Jet again. "I'll meet you at the place you taught me to shift, and we'll walk in together."

"Noon it is." He grabbed her hand and lifted it to his lips. "Don't worry. We'll put him in his place and regain your freedom." After brushing his lips across her palm, he released her with a wry smile.

"Thank you." She trotted a couple of steps, paused, and looked back. "It seems I'm always thanking you for saving my hide." With one more glance, she spun and loped away.

Jet watched her go with a buoyed heart, a momentarily contented inner beast, and a healthy dose of lust.

Garrett watched the expressions flicker on Jet's face—lust, want and happiness. His emotions in turmoil, rampant jealousy smacked him in the chest and wrapped cold fingers around his heart. Frustration raged inside his mind as he realized what his mate had just done, tying them to the errant daughter of Horizon's alpha. Talk about a convoluted puzzle.

"Now would you explain what the hell is going on?" The words clipped out as Garrett struggled to hold onto his waning patience.

Jet pulled his attention from the retreating Rain and met Garrett's gaze. "I ran into Rain five years ago at

Austin's mating ceremony. She had snuck in to watch the event—in human form, no less. Claimed she couldn't shift but didn't let that stop her from doing her damnedest to catch a peek at the happenings. I found her, recognized the name, and escorted her back to her own lands so she could get her teenaged butt home before anyone realized what she did."

"What's this crap about teaching her to shift?"

"I called her on the statement. She tried, but really couldn't do the process. A definite late bloomer. Whatever insanity overcame me, I decided to help by guiding her shift just enough for her to grasp how to get over the last hurdle. She became the little white wolf, thanked me with a lick, and bounded home happy as a lark."

"Okay. Fine. You helped a kid learn to shift. That doesn't make you responsible for her now. Hell's fire. Mating her? What possessed you to say such a thing?" Garrett's gut churned like a cement mixer.

"It's just… I need to help Rain. Protect her."

"What if she's just using you?" He added a bite to his question, a tiny bit compared to the cauldron threatening to erupt inside him at this latest fickle twist.

"Doubtful. I know her, and there's more to her than the painted in the corner person you met tonight."

Garrett rolled his eyes in annoyance. "You're seeing things. Wishing things. Get *this* through your thick skull." He lowered his voice to a snarl. "You heard her. She's using you to defy her father's wishes, to provide a vengeful thorn in his side. She's using you. Period. Against a ruling alpha. And you're stupid enough to let her. How dare you make such a moronic decision without involving me."

Jet's eyes narrowed. His fangs flashed in the sunlight. "First of all, Rain isn't the kind of person you're envisioning. The whole story was the truth, and you can smell lies as easily as I can. She's upset right now, and the prospect of jabbing back at her father is prodding her to outrageous measures." He whispered between them, sounding all the more severe with the soft words spat through gritted teeth. "I've wanted her for the past five years, never forgotten her. And I'll be damned now if I let another male corral her and put his mark on her when fate has obviously made their choice known. She came to me..."

"By accident. Shit, she bowled you over in her headlong run. Not what I would call an intervention by fate." Garrett grumbled right back, not the least cowed with Jet's surly attitude.

"Regardless, I'm taking her as mine."

"What about me?" Garrett hated airing his concerns but he needed to know where he stood.

Jet's shoulders relaxed as he sighed. "You're my mate. I love you and want you. Always will. Having Rain won't change any of that."

"The hell it won't!" Garrett's leash on his temper snapped. "We're committed to one another. What happens to one affects the other. Only you got all pussy happy and decided to let your cock rule your brain. Now, you've invited the daughter of the alpha of a rival pack into our bed. Only a fucking asshole would make such important decisions on the spur of the moment without involving me. Shit, you didn't even mention her name in the three years we've been together."

Jet's mouth opened, but Garrett spoke over him.

"If she was so god damned important to you, then you would have said something. Instead, her name never came up. That's not a fated thing. It's a chicken shit thing to do to me." Garrett spun on his heel and stormed off.

# Chapter Four

Halfway to the opposite side of the Spring Hill Pack territory, Garrett heard his phone ring. Absently noting the caller, he quickly answered, "Hello, Gregori."

"Garrett. How's my son today?"

Gregori, the alpha of the Golden Branch Pack, had been Garrett's mentor growing up. When Garrett's father had tragically died, Gregori had stepped into the shoes, fulfilling the role of parent, even though he teetered on a thousand years old and had many other responsibilities as pack leader to attend to. He referred to Garrett as son, like he did many of the other young men. The gray-headed burly man had always made time for Garrett, had taught him many things, and kept in close touch now that Garrett resided with Jet at the rival Spring Hill pack. While Gregori teased him about mutiny to the enemy, Garrett took the ribbing in his stride.

"If you must know…pissed." As much as he wanted to be civil, the old man would pick up on his tone and prod him until he aired the matter at hand anyway.

He never could hide anything from Gregori, so hardly bothered to try now. Besides, he needed to vent some of the fury riding him hard before he turned back and beat Jet to a pulp.

"What's wrong?"

"Seems Jet stumbled across an old acquaintance and promised to mate her—at once."

"What about you? You didn't say you were accepting her to mate."

"I'm not." Garrett began to pace.

"What's the big hurry, and why is this female so important your chosen one would risk your mate bonds over?"

Garrett puffed out a breath. "She's the daughter of the Horizon alpha. Her father drew the line in the sand. She either finds a mate this weekend or he appoints one for her."

"I see now." Gregori remained silent for a beat. "How better to get back at her father than to mate outside the pack—not only one male, but two?"

"Exactly." Finally, someone understood. Gregori always listened, always saw reason, and could dig out the tiniest detail while pointing out facts and various options. One reason why Garrett looked up to him was because Gregori always leveled with him without tiptoeing around the true issue. He made for a great mentor.

"Well, my son, it appears you have some decisions to make."

"I know." Garrett sighed.

"Are you drawn to the girl in the least?"

He pondered the unexpected question. "She's pretty enough. Her tears disturbed me too—whatever that's worth."

"And you say she's doing this to stick a thorn in her father's side?" Gregori spoke quietly, as if he were busy considering an immensely important opportunity.

"Yes."

"That produces some options for you. Stick by your mate, accept her as your third then decide if you want to keep or reject her once the ruse is over. You may decide she's a good fit."

Garrett groaned. Leave it to his alpha to encourage him to do the noble thing, as much as he wanted to turn his back and leave the girl to her own devices. Unfortunately, Jet had committed them, tying them together at least for the next couple of days.

"If nothing else, you pull one over on the Horizon pack, spend some time screwing the girl then send her on her way."

"I guess."

"When do you stand with her?"

"Tomorrow at noon. We're walking in with her to tell her father in front of the Horizon pack during their festivities."

"Good. Very good." The old voice crackled over the phone line in a low whisper. Only Garrett's extraordinary hearing allowed him to pick up the words.

"Why is it good?"

"Oh, just that making the announcement in front of witnesses might prevent the Horizon alpha from wiggling off the hook. He threw out an ultimatum. Let him stand by it in front of a crowd."

"I see."

"Think about it, son. And keep me updated. I always want to know what's happening in your life."

Garrett swallowed, touched by his obvious concern. "Will do." Clicking off his phone, he stepped into the house, plopped down on the couch, and rested his face in his hands.

How did his life turn so chaotic in a few short minutes? Years of happiness with Jet all boiled down to this moment in time. So what in the world was he going to do?

\* \* \* \*

Jet entered the small cabin he shared with Garrett, spied his mate in the kitchen, his back to the door, smelled the banked anger and hurt feelings, and sighed. His shoulders weighed down with guilt, although not enough to change his mind.

Upon closing the door behind him, he walked quietly across the room, stopping a few feet from Garrett, who stirred a pot slowly. "I know you're angry. You have every right to be." He kept his tone calm and soft, hoping to reach Garrett through reason.

Garrett stiffened, but remained silent.

"I didn't plan for this to happen. Rain was so upset and frightened... I just thought of the idea and jumped on it. No, it's not fair to you and you're right, I was an ass to make the offer without even consulting you in the first place."

"So you've changed your mind?" Garrett asked.

Jet blew out a breath. "No. I intend to follow through. It's up to you if you want to go with me tomorrow or not." He moved closer. "I've wanted Rain from the moment I saw her. When she appeared, I couldn't quell the instant attraction and delight. She's in need and I'll stand up with her, no matter what."

Slowly Garrett turned, his charcoal gray eyes stormy. "If you wanted her from day one, why didn't you speak of her? I've never heard you mention her by name or description before. It seems to me, if she made such a big impression, you would've talked about her now and again."

"I know." Jet sighed. "We hit it off, and all I could think of was you. I didn't forget her, but she moved to a back burner. I kept track of her, though. Asked now and again, listened to any and all rumors. I just couldn't forget her. To be honest, with her living amongst the humans and away from the packs, I figured I had plenty of time to introduce you to the idea, bring about a meeting and see what happened. Unfortunately, because of her father's dictatorship and heavy-handed ways, that didn't happen."

Jet reached out and placed a hand on Garrett's shoulder, wincing at the tension he felt, his heart aching for the pain he caused the man he loved above all others. "I'm sorry. I wish I could go back and do things differently, but I can't. All I can do is move forward, save Rain from her father's folly, and show you that the way I feel about you hasn't changed a bit."

Garrett stared at him for a long moment. "What happens after she declares you her mate? Will she move in here? Go back to her home and life?"

Hearing the underlying hope, Jet resisted the urge to reassure Garrett with unknown facts. "I don't know. She'll probably want to return to her home, but it's something we'll have to discuss."

Jet cupped Garrett's cheek. "I need you. Want you. Love you. But I can't turn my back on her, either." He stroked his thumb across Garrett's smooth lips. "We can get through this together, if we just try."

Garrett released a deep breath, then nuzzled Jet's wrist. "I don't like it, and I still say she's a manipulator who'll drag us under the bus, but I'm not giving up on *us* so easy."

Jet smiled in happiness and relief. "Thank you. I promise to run everything by you first from now on. No more surprises."

The beta nodded. "There's something else you promised me earlier."

"I'd be balls deep in your ass before supper?" Jet arched an eyebrow.

Garrett nodded.

"Maybe you should turn the stove off. It might be a while before we'll get back to the food."

With a flick of his wrist, Garrett turned the heat off and covered the pan with a lid. After taking Jet's offered hand, he led the way to the bedroom.

No sooner had they come to a stop beside the king-sized bed than Jet began tugging at Garrett's shirt, pulling the unwanted garment off and discarding it with a toss. Running his hands over Garrett's chest, Jet paid particular attention to Garrett's nipples, tweaking them into hard pebbles before he trailed his hands downward, following the line of dark hair until he reached the jeans buttons. With teasing slowness, he unlatched each one, watching Garrett's face the entire time.

"How do you want this?"

Garrett's eyes narrowed as he sucked in a breath, forcing Jet's hands against the bulge under the jeans. "Hard and fast. I can't wait any longer." Tugging at his own jeans, Garrett soon pushed them down to puddle at his feet, standing nude before his mate.

Jet wrapped Garrett in his embrace then sealed their lips together, aggressively demanding entrance, then sucking on his tongue with gusto. Garrett responded instantly, grabbing onto Jet's head, holding him close as they tangled tongues in a battle for supremacy and control of the kiss.

Finally, Jet pulled back, drawing in a much needed breath. Jet licked his lips at the sight, never tiring of staring in appreciation at his mate. Absently, he shucked his own clothes, letting them drop to the floor before stepping out of them.

"On the bed."

After spinning on his heel, Garrett climbed on the bed and crawled to the center on hands and knees, wiggling his upturned rear in the process.

A throbbing ache in his burgeoning cock set Jet into motion. Two strides brought him to the bedside table where he found a full tube of lube. After tossing the necessity to the bed, he followed until he knelt behind Garrett. Jet reached out, ran his hands over Garrett's back, down his flanks, and finally over his gorgeous butt.

"You asked. You'll receive."

Scooting back a bit, Jet mirrored his mate's stance, close enough to easily grasp one of Garrett's low hanging testicles in his mouth and begin licking. After hurting Garrett today, Jet strove to make everything up to him, to prove his love and how much Garrett meant to him by his actions.

His mate arched his back and moaned.

Using his lips, Jet pulled on the sensitive flesh, even as he laved the sac. After a moment, Jet released his prize, nuzzled Garrett's balls with his nose then repeated the same treatment to the other ball.

"Stop teasing, damn it," Garrett complained as he rocked slightly.

Garrett's scrotum popped out of Jet's mouth. "Topping from the bottom now?" Nudging higher, Jet ran his tongue along the deep crack between Garrett's cheeks, found the waiting opening and circled the area.

"Oh, shit." Garrett sucked in a breath and pushed back, blatantly asking for more of the same.

Enjoying the foreplay, Jet couldn't help but tease his mate. "Thought you were in a hurry."

Garrett twisted around to meet his gaze. "Not if you're going to rim me. Damn, that's good."

With a knowing chuckle, Jet returned to his task, relishing Garrett's obvious enjoyment. Each lick, kiss and bold swipe over the area brought out more groans and demands from Garrett, arousing him to a fevered pitch. Understanding exactly what the activity did to him, Jet unapologetically strummed Garrett, performing one of his mate's favorite acts in the bedroom. He'd stay there all day, as long as Jet wanted to lick his ass. As much as he wanted to shower Garrett with pleasure, his own cock began to throb with aching need as his already strained control tested the tightly held reins.

Jet reluctantly sat back on his heels, taking a moment to catch his breath. Collecting himself, he smacked Garrett smartly on the rear. "Flat on your stomach."

After latching onto the lube, Jet squirted a large dollop on his hand, then spread the chilly gel over his abundant and needy erection, running his hand up, down, and around until his shaft glistened with readiness.

As instructed, Garrett stretched out across the bed, splayed his legs wide, and turned his head to watch Jet prepare. Gathering more, he spread the lube over his fingers, then around Garrett's rear, sliding in first one, then a second, digit. His gaze flickered between Garrett's beautiful waiting ass and his lover's needy and longing face.

For several minutes, he pleasured Garrett, using his fingers to ready the tight channel for claiming. Soon, he couldn't wait a second longer, and judging by the look on Garrett's face, his mate struggled with his own control.

*Time to mount up and send us both to nirvana.*

Jet slid between Garrett's legs, supporting his weight on his arms. "Reach back and spread those cheeks. Give me an easy target, baby."

Garrett growled but clasped his buttocks and pulled them apart. The action stoked Jet's arousal tenfold. He lined the leaking tip of his cock up with Garrett's anus and pressed forward.

"Ahh." Garrett jerked, released his hold, and fisted the sheets.

Noting the reaction, Jet punched forward, not stopping until he rested completely within his lover. After waiting a few seconds for Garrett to adjust, Jet set a furious pace, only interrupted with an occasional slap to the beta's rear.

"Shit, you feel good. So tight. So hot." He pulled back a few inches and stroked back again, pounding hard, the snug heat lashing at his sensitive dick, showering his body with intense sparks of pleasure. He couldn't get deep enough, plow into Garrett hard enough. His inner wolf clamored for more, howled at the truly dominant position, and demanded Jet take his mate like they both fell headlong into heat.

Good thing his partner preferred sex a bit on the rough side. He couldn't slow or stop if he wanted at this point, way too revved up and close to the pinnacle.

Garrett arched his back, lifted his hips, and whimpered.

"Tell me what you want." The ring of a sound spank echoed through the room. He knew the sting heightened Garrett's arousal as well as his own. The resulting pink marks spurred him on, reminding him of the man beneath, totally at his mercy. Jet savored the moments and dreamed of thousands more with the one man who fired his blood like no other and shared his exuberance for hardcore, sometimes nearly violent couplings.

"Harder. Fuck me harder." Garrett bit out between gasps. "More."

Jet purposely slowed his strokes, pausing with just the mushroomed tip barely resting inside Garrett's opening, now reddened and almost gaping from Jet's dick and his merciless fucking. "Not yet, baby. Not even close."

Garrett answered with a growl, which quickly turned to a moan of blatant need when Jet spanked him twice more. Taking a moment to catch his breath and step back from the edge, Jet sank in, then held steady. He reached under their bodies, found Garrett's sac, and began to tug with exquisite precision, using a milking motion to stretch the tender skin taut.

"Oh, fuck." Garrett started to lift, only to be stopped once more by Jet's strong hand on his back, forcing him back down.

"Hold still, damn it. I'm not done with you yet." He yanked a little less gently in punishment, earning a sharp yip from Garrett.

Jet soothed the area then traced his finger along Garrett's perineum. Back and forth. "You like it rough, don't you?"

"Yessss," Garrett hissed out as he squirmed under Jet's touch.

"What do you want?"

"You to fuck me like a bitch in heat."

A grin cropped up on Jet's face at Garrett's terminology. "I think I can do just that." Jet leaned over, nipped Garrett on the back, then braced himself on his arms, just on the outside of Garrett's shoulders. The new position allowed for maximum thrusting and penetration. Without another word, he set a frantic pace, ensuring each jab not only brushed against Garrett's sweet spot, but reached his farthest depths.

Garrett's channel tightened and constricted as if trying to cling to Jet's dick, to prolong the invasion, to seize Jet's dick and hang onto the delicious length. "Fuck, that's good."

Another whimper, further splaying thighs, and a loud grunt answered.

"Get that ass to work on my cock." Jet gritted the command out between clenched teeth. He adjusted his balance for a moment in order to lay down another hard swat to Garrett's upturned rear.

Garrett cried out, then his core tightened in near desperation. It seemed like he was doing his damnedest to suck Jet's rod not only back inside, but pleading for every drop of cum Jet could possibly provide.

Tingling began at his spine. Throwing everything into the joining, Jet thrust in and out with power. His inner beast surged free, seized control of the mating, and threw them both into a maelstrom of fiery sensations. "More?"

"Yes. Fuck yes." Garrett writhed on the bed, lifted his hips to counter every hard penetration.

"Come, damn you. Come already." Another hard slap landed on Garrett's left cheek, leaving a definite hand print behind. Jet forced his shaft in with difficulty as the knot began to swell. "Garrett..." The name faded into a growl as Jet levered himself over his lover's prone body, found the junction of Garrett's shoulder and neck, and bit down.

"Yesssss..." Garrett's body tightened, bucked then jerked.

Jet surged as deep as possible then held still, unable to move due to the large knot tying them together. Wave after wave of orgasm washed over him, each one accompanied by a release of hot semen into Garrett's willing ass. The channel clenched and clamped, massaging Jet's engorged dick, milking him for all he had.

After releasing his hold, Jet lowered his body over Garrett's, reveling in his extended climax. He settled across Garrett's back, struggling to catch his breath amidst the unending waves of ecstasy rolling through him, each one sending another pulse through his buried dick.

They remained still, caught up in their own rapture, until the last big pulse of seed streamed from Jet's mushroomed tip and his cock began to lose hardness. Only then did he lick over the minor bite wound, intertwine his fingers with Garrett's, and sigh happily. "I love you, Garrett — now and forever."

# Chapter Five

Rain bit her lip, nervously waiting for the two wolf shifter males to arrive. Dozens of thoughts danced through her head, most of all uncertainty over the previously decided upon plan.

What had sounded like the perfect answer to her impossible situation yesterday appeared more like folly today. *What in the world was I thinking? Mating myself to a man I barely know and another I'd never seen before yesterday?* On the flip side, if she called her father's bluff and lost, she might be in the same shoes, finding herself stuck with a man she'd never laid eyes on before. *Scary. Way too scary.*

No. She'd stay the course. *What choice do I really have?* She'd already checked out all the males in Horizon pack over the past twenty-four hours. None of them remotely impressed her, some downright offended her and most simply were easily forgotten. She felt more for Jet's mate, who she'd met briefly before than she did for any of the other males, including the ones she'd known for years. None of the Horizon pack would suit.

Leaving her with Jet's offer. She could accept him and his mate, work something out, and return to her life among the humans. Surely they wouldn't expect her to move in to take over mate duties and warm their bed at night. A shiver ran through her. Maybe the nights wouldn't prove so bad with two such handsome men ready and willing to bestow her with pleasure. They'd run their hands over her body, kiss and lick trails to her most secret places…

Shaking her head, Rain dispelled the daydream. Maybe in an ideal situation where she knew her mates well, she could learn to glory in their claiming. However, she didn't have that luxury. No. Better to avoid sex altogether. Just march up to her father, make the announcement then scurry off until the fireworks died down. Jet and his mate could return to their lives without her as an impediment. His mate would like that.

Garrett. Jet called him Garrett. The name suited him—tall, powerful, full of muscles. Both men could make women drool with a simple smile or come-hither look. To get them both in a single package. *My, oh my.*

Unfortunately, Garrett had balked at the idea of taking her for their mate, even as a ruse. She couldn't blame him. Jet had tossed out the offer, and she'd snatched it up before Garrett could say two words in the matter. She hadn't missed the anger, the hurt that had crossed his face and flashed in his eyes as Jet's noble proposition unwittingly lashed Garrett deeply.

*He must hate me.*

The realization of how much suffering she'd caused him made her heart ache. She didn't like hurting others and had avoided causing others pain at any cost. That hadn't changed since she'd moved away and lived her life with humans. To her, the species didn't matter...the individuals did.

She sighed wearily. As much as she hated the predicament she'd put Jet and Garrett into, she couldn't find another way out. Either she followed through with their suggestion or she returned to her pack alone and waited to see who her father picked. Her shoulders weighed down even more. Her best hope lay in presenting them to her father then going on their merry way. *If* that was possible. A big if.

A musky scent carried to her on the breeze, an aroma she recognized — Jet and Garrett. They topped the small hill and walked steadily toward her.

Rain's heart sped as she sucked in a breath at their appearance. Surely two more handsome men couldn't be found within the whole of their combined packs. Tall, muscular and carrying an air of confidence, they made an outstanding pair — not just in looks but in the sense of power as well. Anyone who challenged them would most likely bite off more than they could chew.

Her nerves crackled. The time had come, and she still hadn't come up with a better solution.

"Rain." Jet stepped close, his gaze searching her face.

She noticed that his expression was full of concern. Turning her attention to Garrett, she found him eyeing her critically, which only added to the burden of her guilt.

"I've looked at all the other men. None of them suit. All night I racked my brain searching for another option. Anything to relieve you of my burden." She stared pointedly at Garrett. "I'm sorry, but I see no way out."

Jet reached out and pulled her against his chest, holding her snugly while petting her hair. "It's okay. I said I wanted to do this, and I still do."

She met Garrett's gaze. "What about Garrett? I don't intend to come between you two."

"I've said my piece and am willing to give it a try." Garrett's gruff tone told her exactly how he felt. Still pissed off but not ready to throw in the towel yet. His body language and expression said he'd fight to the bitter end for Jet, even if he had to personally escort a meddlesome female to another part of the earth. She shivered at the thought of going up against such a foe.

Jet tightened his hold. "Don't worry. We'll work this out." He set her away from him. "First you present us to your father then we'll return to our house and discuss what the future brings."

Rain sighed. "It's not going to be pretty."

Garrett snorted.

Jet's lips twitched. "I have a feeling, with you, nothing ever will be."

"Hey!" She frowned. "I'm not that bad."

"Just lead the way, lady. It's hot, and I'm not getting any younger," Garrett grumbled under his breath.

She nodded briefly and started down the all too familiar path, guilt eating at her every step of the way. "Don't worry, I'm not going to hold you guys to anything. I'm independent and more than capable of taking care of myself."

"Which says shit about the mess you dragged us in."

Rain cringed at Garrett's surly tone. She blew out a breath. "I'm sorry. Again."

"It's going to be okay." Jet shot Garrett a quick glare.

"It's not like I wanted this to happen." Rain's voice grew higher. "I didn't even want to come back for this dang event. But, my parents had other plans."

"Sucks being the daughter of an alpha pair, huh?" Garrett sneered.

"You have no idea." She lifted her chin. "Walk in my shoes for a day before you judge."

"Fine. As soon as you walk in mine, lady."

Jet sliced his hand through the air. "Enough bickering already. We've got to present a united front because it's just about show time."

Rain nodded and slowed her strides. Just ahead stood a gathering of Horizon pack members, including her father. "Here goes nothing." She made a beeline for him.

He turned his attention to her, lifted his nose to scent the air then frowned. His expression didn't deter her in the least. Instead, she marched up to stand toe to toe with her father.

Lifting her chin, she chose her words carefully. "Father. You said I had to choose a mate this weekend or you would choose one for me."

"Yes."

Curious pack members gathered around, eagerly listening to the conversation. Rain ignored them, though she reveled in their presence. With witnesses, she'd skewer her father on his own stick. Her mother hurried over, her face slightly pale, even as she chewed her bottom lip.

"And you said the only requirement was he had to be an adult male wolf shifter."

"Yes?" His eyebrows furrowed as if picking up a small deceit.

"You also promised if I found a man who met those requirements, there'd be no questions asked."

"Again, yes. If you've found a man, then present him already."

Rain bit back a grin, half turned, and gestured toward Jet and Garrett, who'd been hanging back as to avoid drawing attention. Now, they came forward to stand on either side of Rain.

"Father, may I present my new mates, Jet and Garrett."

Her father's face turned bright red as he glanced at the men with a scowl. "They aren't of our pack, young lady."

"I know. But that wasn't part of the agreement, was it?"

His hands fisted as a vein throbbed in his head. "A daughter of mine isn't mating some damn Spring Hill whelp."

"Spring Hill whelp?" Jet arched an eyebrow.

Garrett narrowed his eyes and flashed his fangs but remained mute.

Rain growled and didn't budge. "Again. It's not your choice. I fulfilled my part of the bargain. End of story."

"I forbid this." He bellowed with rage. "You *will* obey."

"You can't do a damn thing about it, Father. You forced me into this. So deal." With those words, she twined her hands with her new mates.

A collective gasp from the onlookers carried across the area. Thick tension appeared like a dark storm cloud about to burst—just like her more than difficult father.

Rain ignored them, glimpsed the odd expression on her mother's face then spun around.

"Mark my words. You're going to regret this. All of you." Her father bit off each word.

Holding on tightly to her mates and refusing to glance back, she turned and walked proudly away, bracketed by the new men in her life.

A shiver washed over Rain as she left the Horizon pack lands and entered Spring Hill territory. Before, the crossing of boundary lines had never bothered her. This time her gut clenched with the significance.

The confrontation with her father had left her rattled, yet oddly proud of her victory. *Teach him to try to run my life.* Now, thanks to her new two mates, she had a bright future. Hopefully.

"Thank you both. I'm afraid if you weren't there, he might have taken more drastic measures."

"He was definitely pissed off." Garrett walked on her left, his long strides eating up the distance easily.

"Big time. Good thing you reminded him ahead of time of the promise. He had no way to counter you, especially in front of half your pack." Jet picked up a pebble and skipped the rock ahead of them. "I don't think it's wise to return there."

"I'll stay away for now," she agreed but couldn't promise to never return. All her family lived there, plus her car and the supplies she brought for the weekend remained on Horizon property. Sadness filled her at the thought of never seeing them again. "Until things have a chance to calm down. Father will eventually accept my decision."

"I'm not so sure of that." Garrett shook his head. "Seems to me he'll never welcome outside wolf shifters."

"He rarely has before, but there's always a chance he might this time." Rain forced hope and conviction into her voice. In truth, she considered the same thoughts and couldn't help but worry. *In my bid for freedom, have I ostracized myself from my family anyway?*

"I guess the question right now is what you're going to do and where you intend to live." Jet grabbed her arm to help her over a particularly steep and rocky patch.

"I'm not sure, to be honest. Originally I'd thought to pull off the ruse then simply return to my home and business."

"And, now?" Jet asked.

"Now, I'd like your input. As much as you both have done for me, your opinion and suggestions count—more than you know."

Garrett gritted his teeth and clenched his fists. All this fiasco, just to get back at her father, just as he'd figured out and warned mule-headed Jet. The selfish little chit. Didn't she know what privilege being a mate entailed? Her words and actions threw mud on the sanctity of the bond he and Jet shared. After they stepped up for her, she insulted them with her choice of words.

As much as he wanted to load the girl up in her vehicle and send her on her way, Jet would balk. Besides, he'd promised to give Rain a chance. From what he'd witnessed so far, he'd make sure the chance remained small and short. No way would he spend the rest of his extended life catering to the willful spoiled brat and master manipulator.

Sure, he'd listened to her apologies, seen the anxiety their decision caused. Yet, he didn't believe her for more than a split second. Rain held her own interests at heart and would follow through with what benefited her the most. Damn bitch.

*Why can't Jet see her true colors? Because he's thinking with his dick.*

They'd both been with other men and women before they'd found one another. Hell, Garrett was open to just about anything but he drew the line at Rain.

Whatever Jet saw in her, Garrett didn't have a clue. All he knew was somehow, someway, he needed to either convince Jet to let Rain return to her own life, without them, or to open the other man's eyes to the blistering situation she'd stuck them with.

He wasn't without compassion. Sure, he'd buck the system too if his alpha demanded he choose a mate immediately. However, there were dozens of single males all eager to accept Rain into their home and bed. She could have easily chosen one of them instead of doing her best to screw up *his* life.

Puffing out a breath, he grappled for patience. Jet cared for the girl. He'd give her enough rope to hang herself with. Then his mate would see the truth and toss Rain out on her rear.

Jet hurried ahead. "Austin?"

A tall dark-headed man stopped and turned around. Jet's brother and one of the alphas of Spring Hill pack. Garrett had met him on several occasions, genuinely liked the man and respected him for his leadership role in a tolerant, yet powerful wolf pack.

"I want you to meet someone. This is Rain. Our new mate."

Austin's eyebrows shot up as surprise flashed across his face. "This was sudden." Stepping closer, he appraised Rain carefully, then held out a hand. "Pleased to meet you, finally."

Her eyebrows knitted. "Finally?"

Austin grinned. "Well, I would have met you at my mating ceremony, but my overprotective brother here whisked you away before I had a chance."

Rain's cheeks blossomed red. "Does everyone know about that incident?"

"Yep."

"Wonderful. You all must think I'm such a twit."

Austin met Garrett's gaze before returning to the female. "Never that. Bold and reckless, maybe."

"Uh huh." She sighed wearily.

Garrett snorted. Why did everyone cater to the girl? Couldn't they see what he saw? One day soon, she'd screw up, and he'd be the first one to kick her rump off Spring Hill land. Reining in his anger, he remained mute.

"Come along. I'll introduce you to the rest of the pack." Austin gestured for them to follow.

Garrett frowned. "We were just going to take her home. Seems we have lots to discuss."

Jet and his bother both turned to Garrett. Finally, the alpha shook his head. "You have time for a casual introduction. Besides, it'll save explanations later."

Grumbling to himself, Garrett paused for a moment, watching the others stride toward the center of the pack meeting grounds. The last thing any of them needed was for Rain to endear herself to other pack members, spinning them all in her web of deceit. Yet, he couldn't refuse an outright command from Austin. Promising to watch the chit extra closely, he followed along.

# Chapter Six

"Come on in." Jet held the door to the cabin open until Rain and Garrett both stepped through. He shared a long look with Garrett and felt a chill wash over him. Garrett wasn't pleased at all. Not with the handling of Rain's situation, not with her in general, not with the impromptu introduction to their pack, and certainly not with her entering their home as a new mate, their supposed third.

He'd always known Garrett possessed a jealous streak, but he'd never thought to see the blatant signals of such an emotion in the other man's body language. If only Garrett could see what he saw, understand what he did. Yet, no matter how much he'd tried to explain, Garrett had his selective hearing turned up high and blinders over his eyes. No matter. With time, he'd learn more about Rain, come to realize she was not the wily manipulator Garrett thought she was, and perhaps accept her into their relationship with open arms.

*Yeah, right. Maybe in the next five hundred years or so.*

With a sigh, Jet followed the others into the spacious living room, closing the door behind him. Garrett would just have to put his feelings aside for a while until they figured out what to do next.

"Have a seat." Jet gestured to the sofa.

Once Rain plopped down in the far corner, he chose the opposite while Garrett remained standing, a statement not missed by Jet.

"Let's discuss this. We've formally announced matehood."

Rain nodded. "Our packs will view the mating as valid and extend the customary benefits and expectations that go along with the relationship."

"But where does that leave us?" Garrett cut through the clutter right down to the very basics.

"That's up to Rain." Jet met her gaze. "We're not going to hold you hostage. If you choose to return to your home among the humans, we won't insist you remain here. However, I'd like it if you hung around at least a few days, get to know us, meet the rest of Spring Hill Pack. See what life could be like if you stayed permanently."

She glanced at Garrett then back to Jet. "Will my being here change anything?"

"Change anything how?" Garrett asked.

"What if you want to try out another person for potential mate? Would my presence interfere in that?" Her words came out as a whisper.

"Why should it? This pack openly accepts all relationships. If we chose to add another, we'd do so—with or without you." Garrett laid down the law.

Jet jumped in, hoping to ease the tension and find common ground between his two mates. "By staying, you'll see what life can be here. We're not asking you to become a maid, to slave away. Simply remain as a guest, experience a different wolf shifter culture. See if you like it here. After that, you can do whatever you please. Leave. Stay. Or something in between. We're not going to cage you."

If only Garrett would get to know her better. Perhaps in a few days, he'd chill enough to recognize Rain's goodness. *Yeah, and the Spring Hill and Horizon packs will someday become best allies, too – after a thousand years of turmoil – and pigs will grow wings and take to the skies.*

One way or another, he'd make this work. He had to. After finding his two mates, he wasn't about to let them go because of a rough first impression and soured feelings. Stubborn determination steeled his resolve.

"So will you stay?" He stared at Rain and waited.

"Yes."

Relief washed over him. Step one completed. A quick glance found Garrett scowling at her answer. As much as he wanted to shake his mate, he refrained, hoping with some time together, he might settle down, see Rain as Jet saw her. Patience ruled the day.

"She's not sleeping in our bed." Garrett threw out the first pitch.

"I'll have you know, I had no intention of sleeping in the same bed with you. Geez. I'm not a slut or desperate for your bodies." Rain threw her hands up. "Men are so arrogant. Just because there's a woman around, they think she can't have a mind of her own, decent morals and a will to control herself and her life." Rain glared at Garrett.

Garrett didn't back down an inch. "I don't think you're desperate, I think you're a conniving manipulator."

Rain gasped.

Jet stepped between them, scowling. "That's enough. Both of you." He reached out a hand toward them both, ensuring they kept their distances. "Rain can sleep in the spare bedroom or on the couch. I certainly had no plans to insist upon a traditional claiming." He turned to stare at Garrett. "I get that you're majorly pissed off. My fault. Take it out on me, not Rain. She had no control over the situation and only did what she had to in order to avoid the traumatic experience of having a mate she didn't want forced on her. I offered. She accepted. We'll work out details later. Until then, back off and give her a chance."

Garrett lifted his lip, showing a long, wicked fang. "Fine. But don't get all nasty when I say I told you so."

Jet's tension ebbed a hair when he backed down. Garrett normally walked the laid-back path, full of laughter and play. However, when his hackles were raised, he'd take on a grizzly in order to protect and preserve what he felt was right. Jet often questioned whether Garrett disguised his true alpha wolf-self. Certainly, he showed quite a few alpha tendencies, too many for an average beta. Normally, Jet found the combination amusing and reveled in the package that made up Garrett. Today, Garrett's near challenge of Rain tested Jet's tolerance.

"Fine." Rain's shoulders sank. "I know you don't believe me, but I'm sorry to put you through this and really do appreciate everything you both have done for me." She looked from the floor to meet Garrett's gaze. "I promise I'll stay out of the way, pull my own weight, and be the least burden I can—just for a few days—to give us a chance to figure out the future. I've got extra clothes packed in my car. I'll retrieve them later." With those words, she headed down the hall, stuck her head in their bedroom then continued one more door down. She stepped in and disappeared from sight.

Jet turned to Garrett. "I've never asked you for anything. I'm asking you this. Just get to know her. Let go of your bias and start over with a blank slate."

Garrett growled. "For you, I'll try. But don't expect a single thing more." He spun around and strode out, slamming the storm door behind him.

*No one said this is going to be easy.*

"I'm sorry." Guilt weighed Rain's shoulders down as she emerged into the hallway. Her gaze sought Jet, finding his face pinched and his body taut with tension. "Maybe I should just leave."

His black gaze locked on her. "No. Just because Garrett has a stick up his ass doesn't mean we give up so quickly. He'll come around, once he has time to settle down and see the forest through the trees."

"I'm not so sure he'll ever come around." She lowered her chin. "He hates me." Why the sentiments of a near stranger bothered her so much, she didn't know, but the idea of such animosity from Garrett hit her like a kidney punch.

Jet reached out and placed his index finger under her chin. He lifted until she looked at him. "He doesn't hate you, Rain. He's just jealous and upset with me over the quick changes in our life. Erroneously, he places the blame on you. I'll make him see the truth. It'll just take some time." He kissed her nose. "Can you be patient with both of us? Give him time to reconsider his feelings?"

She nodded. "I'll try. As long as he doesn't get physical."

Jet's eyebrows furrowed. "Physical? Do you expect him to attack you?"

Rain swallowed. "It wouldn't be the first time a male grew angry enough with a female and released his anger in such a manner."

"That's bullshit." Jet spat out the words, his eyes snapped as his mouth flattened into a thin line. "Anyone who hits a female is nothing but a damn lowlife, the worst kind." He blew out a breath, took her hand and lifted her palm for a brief caress with his lips. "Listen up, Rain. I promise you that no one here will ever lift a hand to you in anger. Not me, not Garrett. No one in this entire pack."

"How can you make a promise for dozens of others?" She tilted her head in question but didn't pull her hand away from the small show of affection, which sent butterflies dancing through her stomach.

"Because our pack doesn't allow such violence. Granted, we're far from perfect, and shifters break the laws now and again, but that kind of behavior isn't tolerated."

"In Horizon—"

He shushed her with a finger over her lips. "Sweetheart, you're no longer in Horizon pack. Spring Hill lands, Spring Hill pack. Spring Hill laws. You're more than safe here."

His words sank in. She was free—from her father's overbearing, mulish demands and from the constant watching from Horizon members. Every shifter she had met today had been nothing but curious and pleasant, seemingly interested in her, her story, and genuine in their offer of friendship. They had eased her nerves greatly and gave her hope for the future. Hope with her mates in her new pack.

For the first time, she considered her home among the humans and found parts of her life lacking. She missed being around others of her own species—the ability to shift whenever and wherever the urge hit, to race through the hills without fear of someone reporting a scary beast on the loose. To be surrounded by people who understood her basic nature. Maybe, just maybe...

She mentally shook her head. How could she forget the mountainous obstacles in her way? As caring and attentive as Jet had been, Garrett matched him in the opposite. While Jet spoke of his faith that the beta would come around, she wasn't about to hold her breath. She'd glimpsed too much turmoil, too much pain in the man's eyes to believe he'd return with a renewed, positive attitude toward her. Nothing short of a miracle or divine intervention would make Garrett see her as less than a major threat to his happiness with Jet.

Her father remained a thorn in her side. Sure, she'd outmaneuvered him by choosing mates from another pack—a temporary fix to an impossible situation. His rage wouldn't abate for a long time—possibly never—leaving her walking on hot coals around him, if he'd even allow her to return for a visit. She might have succeeded in thwarting his order but ended up with the same result—forced removal from her family pack.

"Rain?"

She blinked and focused back on Jet, finding an expression of concern on his face.

"Don't worry so much. I know things appear difficult right now, but we'll get through this."

She nodded and wrapped her arms around his neck in a much needed hug. He pulled her tighter into his embrace, simply holding her for a long moment. "You're mine, and I'm not losing you."

The words sent a flutter of excitement through her, along with a healthy dose of uncertainty.

"Why did you want me for a mate?" she whispered against his ear.

"Because from the first moment we met, I knew you'd enrich my life."

His words soothed her and provided support and confidence, which she'd sorely lacked since this ordeal began.

Swallowing back tears, she stepped away. As much as she would have loved to stand there all day comforted by Jet, her pride demanded she lift her chin, plod along, and prevail. Wolves valued strength and courage, not pity parties and tears.

"I'll see about fixing something for supper."

"You don't have to. Remember, you're the guest."

She halfway grinned. "A guest who needs to stay busy and earn her keep."

Jet smiled. "Whatever you want."

\* \* \* \*

"Supper's ready." Rain plunked the last piece of fried chicken onto the platter. Already the dining table held a handful of side dishes, the plates, silverware, and glasses filled with ice tea. After scooting items around, she found a space just big enough for the chicken.

"What smells so good?" Garrett ambled in, sniffing the air.

Rain watched him warily, not quite comfortable in his presence since he made his views of her so openly known.

"Rain cooked. A smorgasbord." Jet gestured to the table.

Garrett's gaze lifted from the food to her face. "Why?"

She shrugged. "I don't mind cooking. Besides, I like to earn my keep."

"Uh huh." He walked to the sink and washed his hands.

Jet plopped down and picked up a fork. "My stomach's been growling for the past hour. I know you're hungry as well." He looked at Garrett. "Anything interesting on patrol?"

"No." Garrett shook his head and sat down.

"Rain, come over here and eat while it's hot." Jet stabbed a chicken leg with his fork and dropped it onto his plate.

Dutifully, she slid into one of the remaining empty chairs and sipped her tea. Her stomach knotted with nerves and regrets as she watched the two men.

Garrett dug in, shooting her a look ripe with animosity. Obviously, he didn't care for her spending so much time alone with Jet. She couldn't begrudge him for his jealousy or anger at her interruption in their lives. Yet, as much as she racked her brain for ways to prove herself to him, nothing clicked. Words hadn't worked. Actions were necessary. Only she didn't know what those might be.

Emotions boiled up, and a lump formed in her throat. The tension at the table became enough to choke. "I'm going for a run."

She replaced her tea glass on the table and quickly stood.

Both men blinked at her.

"You haven't eaten." Jet pointed out the obvious.

"I'm not hungry."

"Don't tell me you poisoned the food," Garrett said in a grumpy tone.

Her mouth fell open on a gasp. "No, you toad, I didn't poison the food. I can't believe you're accusing me of such a thing." Spinning on her heel, she marched to the entranceway.

"Rain..." Jet's voice followed her out of the front door.

Pausing only long enough to shed her clothes on the front porch, she quickly shifted into her furry form and took off at a dead run into the night.

# Chapter Seven

Garrett stepped out of the door just as the first rays of daylight streamed across the wooded land. As he took a moment to enjoy the view, his nose picked up a familiar scent. He swiveled his head to find Rain in wolf form sleeping at the edge of the porch, her back against the wall of the house.

After she'd rushed out last night, Jet had released his anger on Garrett. By the time the lecture had finished, he'd wanted to either throttle Rain, her father, or the whole damn Horizon pack for throwing such a clog in his happiness. At the same time, a modicum of doubt entered his mind. Jet believed totally in the girl. While she certainly could be pulling the wool over Jet's eyes, a tiny possibility of innocence remained. Jet had pointed out facts last night that had stuck in Garrett's mind. Maybe he'd been harsh on Rain. If she turned out to be the angel Jet claimed, Garrett would apologize on his knees if he had to. That was a big if.

His attention centered on the solid white wolf stretched out on her side—cute and sweet. For one ridiculous moment, he longed to walk over and stroke her fur, find out if the coat felt as soft and fluffy as it appeared. Just as quickly, he discarded the idea. While Jet had pointed out some positive ideas, Garrett wasn't ready to accept her as readily as his mate had. Not until time passed and everything settled down with no further drama. Then, and only then, would he even begin to consider Rain as a potential mate.

She sighed in her sleep, drawing his appraisal once more. Why she didn't come back in and sleep in a more comfortable bed, he didn't have a clue.

*To each their own.*

With a shrug, he jogged down the porch steps, hung a sharp right, and headed to the perimeter. His turn at patrol, a task he took seriously.

As he approached the boundary with Horizon land, the stench of blood and death snared his attention. Following his acute sense of smell, he picked up the pace until he nearly stumbled over a body, then rushed over. The man lay face down on the dusty earth, blood covered his torn clothes and puddled under him. Garrett recognized the scent of the individual, another lower ranking beta who worked in the security department, assigned to the same task as he. However, another lingering aroma tickled his senses, teased him with familiarity but remained elusive as to the actual source. He'd smelled the particular scent before but simply didn't have enough to connect the dots.

Glancing around, anger filled his gut. Footprints and paw prints were scattered all around, the only evidence he found of the killer.

*Senseless. Absolutely senseless.* His gaze searched over their rival's territory, finding more tracks that led back to Horizon's main living areas.

After grabbing the deceased man, Garrett turned him over, sucking in a breath at the brutal results of an attack. Tears in the victim's clothing revealed deep gouges in the flesh beneath. If the man had tried to protect himself, Garrett found no evidence of defensive wounds, as if the man had been taken by surprise and paid the ultimate price for his inattention.

A piece of white paper spotted with blood caught his eye. He pulled the note from the pin clasping it to the man's shirt.

After unfolding the paper, he gasped at the message. *"Due to your audacity, there will be more."*

Given the situation with Rain and her enraged father, all fingers seemed to point to Spring Hill's neighbors. Speaking of the female, he recalled she'd spent the night running—alone. Certainty of her guilt settled in his gut, despite what the note said. Fury washed over him as he thought about the murderess in *his* home with *his* mate.

Wasting no time, he whipped out his cell phone and called in the body. Let the investigative team begin their work. Once they arrived, he'd be free to go check on Jet and inform him of the possible killer living under their roof.

\* \* \* \*

The ringing of Garrett's phone drew his focus as he watched the investigative team processing evidence.

After checking the caller ID, he immediately answered. "Gregori." Garrett turned on his heel and started walking back toward home, ensuring privacy for his conversation with his alpha.

"Garrett. How's your situation coming along? Have you either welcomed the female or sent her packing?"

"Neither." Garrett entered the house and found a nearby chair. He sat down, eager to tell his problems to an understanding ear. "And things have taken a big downturn."

"Now what?"

"It seems Horizon is furious over Jet and Rain's ruse. They've killed a Spring Hill pack member."

"That sounds serious." The old alpha muttered under his breath.

"It could mean all-out warfare over this damn mating, just to avoid her father appointing a male. Absolutely ridiculous."

"Agreed."

"Is Spring Hill going to retaliate?"

Garrett shrugged then remembered his alpha couldn't see the gesture over the phone. "I don't have a clue. The body was just found, so the pack alphas are in a meeting now to decide the next step."

"Such a waste. Just for a female." He paused for a long moment. "Seems to me she's part of some sort of setup. Infiltrate the pack, search for weaknesses, then report back to her father. The little spy could be setting you up for a bloody takeover."

"The same female who pushed her way into our home and into Jet's good graces." He couldn't keep the anger and frustration from his voice.

"He just brought her home like a stray puppy?"

"Yes." His pride stung as did his deep feelings still in turmoil over the huge monkey wrench named Rain who'd been tossed into the middle of a smooth-running relationship.

"Son, it sounds like you need to grow some balls and put your foot down. Fight for your mate. Don't let that conniving girl take Jet from you."

"Working on it." He sighed and ran a hand through his hair. His alpha wasn't telling him anything he hadn't already thought a dozen times himself.

"Good. Someone needs to interrogate that girl. Sounds like she has some manipulation and dark secrets on her plate."

"It could just be coincidence."

Gregori snorted. "Boy, there's no such thing."

Garrett soaked in his alpha's words as he opened the front door to his cabin.

"Keep me posted about the murder and possible retaliation. I need to prepare our pack if things get ugly."

"Will do."

Garrett's old pack—Golden Branch—a ragtag group of previously ousted wolf shifters who'd come together in order to survive and fulfill their social needs. While small, they could be a formidable force if pushed. Gregori would make sure the members stood ready in case any fighting spilled over into their much smaller territory. He'd look after the group, just like he still looked over Garrett, as a wise old father might.

*What am I going to do?* Garrett shook his head and tilted it back far enough to stare at the ceiling. After years of happiness, his world had turned upside down with the addition of Rain. Now, not only he struggled, but two packs would be discussing the distinct possibility of coming to blows over one person. No one was worth the high cost of lives. No one.

Forcing his attention back to a more pressing matter, he punched in Jet's number, hoping the alpha wasn't in the middle of a screwing session with Rain. *He damned well better not be.*

Considering most wolf shifters weren't prudes when it came to sex, a pair in lust wouldn't hesitate to get down and dirty anywhere — the woods, a car, behind a house, or even in the middle of the park. He and Jet had done so before. No big jump to expect Jet and Rain to find a slice of heaven in the middle of a clearing, regardless of prying eyes.

"Hey, Garrett." His mate sounded chipper and upbeat, probably from spending who knows how long in the sack with the bane of Garrett's life.

"We've got a problem."

"What kind of problem?"

"Get your ass back home, and I'll tell you." His voice came out as a stern demand. He didn't care if Jet liked the tone or bristled because a beta dared order him around.

"What's so fucking important that I have to race back there?" Jet clipped off each and every word.

"Murder."

"What the shit?"

"You heard me. I just found one of our guards dead just across our shared border with Horizon Pack."

"Damn."

"Yeah. It gets worse. Seems the killer left a note. 'Due to your audacity, there will be more'."

"Holy hell."

\* \* \* \*

Jet paced the floor, unable to dispel the sinking feeling in his gut since Garrett had told him the news. "I don't understand. Sure, Rain's father was pissed off.

We get that. But to murder another pack's member and risk all-out war? That's insane."

Garrett leveled his gaze at Rain. "Sounds like the acorn doesn't fall far from the tree." He sounded snarky to his own ears, but he couldn't get past the facts. Rain had begun this whole mess and bore responsibility for the death of one of their friends, whether she personally executed him or not.

Rain flinched but didn't protest the label. "I can't see Father ordering such a thing. We've had an uneasy truce with Spring Hill forever. Why break it now?"

"Because you called his bluff and made him look bad in front of his pack?" Garrett answered.

"No. There's got to be more to this than we're seeing." Jet tapped his lips with one long finger.

Garrett eyed Rain carefully. "You were out all night. Alone. No alibi."

Rain gasped. "I didn't kill anyone!"

Jet growled deep in his throat. "How dare you accuse her of murder!"

Garrett narrowed his eyes, his gaze flickering between them. "You might not have actually attacked the man, but it seems awfully convenient that you were missing all night when the murder took place. Maybe you were the distraction, the accomplice."

Jet stepped forward immediately. Rain grabbed his arm and held him back. "I realize you think I'm the devil incarnate but don't let your jaded view of me turn you into a fool for linking unrelated events together." Her voice came out soft and steady with just enough of a bite to show her anger. "Let me talk to my parents. I'm sure they're as confused over this as we are," Rain offered. "I need to fetch my SUV anyway."

Jet slowly opened and closed his hands to physically release the tension from his body. He stared down at Rain and pondered her request. She should be safe enough during daylight and with both packs aware of her location.

Finally, he nodded. "Go see what they have to say. I'll talk to our leaders and see if they can enlighten us further."

"Okay. I'll be back later." She glanced pointedly at Garrett then headed out of the cabin.

As soon as she managed to be out of earshot, Jet unloaded. "Back off Rain."

Garrett didn't even blink. "Too much coincidence. Let me guess. The scent of pussy has your dick so hard you don't have any blood left for your brain."

Fury sparked inside Jet as he turned on his mate. He surged forward, shoving Garrett against the living room wall. His forearm lodged under the beta's chin. Slowly, Jet added pressure, enough to cut off the airflow for a couple of moments.

"I've tolerated more than enough of your bullshit. Yeah, I chose her for a mate to help her out of a sticky situation. Yes, I didn't ask you ahead of time. Call me an asshole, rant if you will, but you *will* cease the childish surliness with Rain." He waited a moment while Garrett met his gaze unflinchingly. "If you *ever* accuse her of murder or being an accessory to the crime, you and I will have a big problem." Gradually Jet backed off, allowing his mate to breathe normally again.

Never in their years together had he been forced to take such an alpha stance with Garrett. He hated to do so now, but enough was enough.

Rage crossed Garrett's face before he schooled his expression into a disgusted scowl. "Fine. I'll only be too glad to say I told you so when I get to the bottom of this case." Standing tall, Garrett lifted his chin then strode out of the front door.

Jet scrubbed his face and growled, even as he processed one tidbit he gained from the whole violent interaction. Garrett had never backed down, groveled, or even lowered his gaze. Instead, his pissed off expression had dared Jet to do his worst.

For as long as Jet had known Garrett, he held beta status, though a high ranking one. Now, Garrett's behavior nagged at Jet, forcing him to recognize the obvious signs.

Garrett might have started out as a beta, but somewhere along the line, he'd risen to pure alpha.

*Just another monkey wrench in our quickly derailing relationship.*

With a weary sigh, Jet headed out, needing some fresh air and time to absorb this new discovery.

# Chapter Eight

Rain rapped on the door to her father's office, waiting patiently for him to acknowledge her. After their difficult last meeting, she vowed to tread carefully and avoid upsetting him any more than necessary. As far as she was concerned, she had her mates — the episode had reached completion, so they could hopefully patch their relationship to a more civil level.

Finally, he glanced up, then resumed poring over the papers before him. "Come in." He would have scented her long before she knocked, so the wait proved to be a meddlesome thorn in her side as probable payback.

After stepping into the room, she found the chair across from her father, sat down, and crossed her feet at the ankles. "Father, I have news."

"About your ridiculous choice of mates? Spare me the details."

His surly tone pricked her annoyance. Reminding herself of the importance of the matter, she lifted her chin. "No. It's about a murder. On Horizon land."

The alpha's head snapped up. "What murder?"

"One of the Spring Hill patrols found a dead pack mate just over the line of Horizon's territory. The initial impression is Horizon had something to do with the man's brutal death."

"What the hell? You know better than that. Why would I order a Spring Hill shifter to be killed? Granted, there's no love lost between our two packs, but there's no reason to upset the volatile truce between us."

"People know you're upset over my choice of mates and have started throwing out possible scenarios. Namely that, in the heat of the moment, you might have thrown out an order of revenge."

"That's personal. Pack business is separate. I would never risk the safety of the other members because my own daughter stabbed me in the back."

She flinched and sucked in a breath. Her father didn't mince words. At least he told the truth. He didn't bear responsibility for the untimely demise. Relief coursed through her, quickly tempered by his scalding and hurtful words. Of course, he'd be stubborn enough to hold a grudge for a few centuries. Unable to change his way of thinking, she focused on the matter at hand.

"I'm sure Spring Hill alphas are awaiting your call to figure out what's going on and how to prevent someone else from dying in the process." Her level tone belied the volcano erupting in her gut with chaotic emotions, anger, and frustration at the core.

"I'll call them all right. No one blames this bullshit on me." He reached for his cell phone and began searching through the contact list.

Rain stood up and turned to go.

"Rain?"

She waited for the other shoe to drop. "Yes?"

"Thank you for bringing this to my attention."

"You're welcome." She worried her lip for a second, then blurted out the question demanding an answer. "Will you ever accept me or the men I chose?"

He stared at her a long moment before blowing out a breath. "I don't know."

She nodded. "Fair enough." With one more look, she hurried out of the door and into the fresh air of morning. While he didn't apologize for his words or actions, at least he recognized civility in her efforts and left the door open for future interactions. A baby step in the right direction.

With a lightly renewed sense of hope, she trotted to the parking area where she'd left her car.

Couple of days. She sighed and kicked her distracted brain into gear. She needed to call Autumn and ask her to take over for a while. Just until she could iron things out and return to her regularly scheduled life.

She palmed her phone, punched in the number, then waited.

Autumn answered on the second ring. "Hello?"

"Hey. It's me."

"Rain. How's it going? Are you on your way home?"

"No. Not yet. Something's come up and I need to hang out at home for a few days." She so much wanted to confide the real happenings to her friend, but dared not. While Autumn wouldn't go on a wolf hunt, she couldn't trust her friend not to let anything slip by accident.

"Oh, no. What's wrong?" Autumn's tone filled with worry.

"Nothing big. I just need some time to iron things out with my parents is all." Rain bit her lip with the lie.

"Don't tell me they lined up a suitor for you." Autumn chuckled.

Rain decided a smidgen of the whole picture wouldn't hurt. After all, she needed a good excuse for taking days away from work without Autumn starting to fret or grow concerned. "Well, they might have tried, but I beat them to the punch."

"You met a guy?"

"Uh huh."

"Is it serious?"

"Uh huh." Considering they were sort of mated, serious was an understatement.

"That's wonderful!" Happiness came across through Autumn's voice.

"Thanks. There's some things that we need to figure out before I come home. If you don't mind watching the shop for me...?"

"No problem. Besides, it's about time you took a vacation."

"Thanks. I'll let you know something when we get things figured out." Right now that felt like the twelfth of never.

"Take your time. Really."

"Okay. Call if you need anything."

"I'll be fine. Just go enjoy that man of yours." With that, Autumn disconnected.

Rain blew out a breath. She hated lying to her friend, but had no choice.

*Enjoy that man of yours.* Autumn's words replayed through her mind.

*If only it were that easy.*

With a sigh, she set out on her way once more.

\* \* \* \*

Straightening her back, Rain quietly opened the front door of Jet and Garrett's cabin, before quietly shutting it behind her. As much as she needed to report her father's view on the murder and his intentions, she almost dreaded returning to the home of her mates. *Temporary mates.* She'd decided to return to her house and business among the humans in a few days, despite Jet's efforts to make her feel like a special guest in his home. While she might have been able to live with Jet, absorb his attentions and affections, she couldn't see Garrett ever seeing her as more than a threat to his relationship with Jet.

She couldn't blame Garrett for his concerns, considering the speed and suddenness of this whole convoluted ordeal. Garrett had simply lashed out at the person he held responsible and moved to protect the man he loved. Maybe if the situation had been different, she would've seen another side to him. Unfortunately, she'd never know.

Hearing a muffled grunt, she furrowed her eyebrows and stealthily walked down the short hallway, stopping just outside Jet and Garrett's bedroom. She scented both men and something else — sex.

She peeked around the corner then bit back a gasp at the sight. Jet lay flat on his back on the bed while Garrett knelt over him, his back to Rain. As she watched, he lifted up a few inches, revealing Jet's erection, then slid back down, lodging the thick shaft deep inside his body again. Although she couldn't see the whole picture, the sheer size and girth of Jet's member — which she could see each time Garrett lifted—both amazed and excited her. How did Garrett take such a large erection? A shudder raced through her.

As if in answer, Garrett picked up the pace. Up. Down. He threw his head back, growled low then circled his hips.

Rain blinked, transfixed by the erotic scene right before her eyes. She should turn and leave, at least return to the living room and wait for them to finish, dress, and come looking for her. Instead, she stood still and stared, unable to make her feet move as she took in the glorious view of the two men wrapped up in intimate pleasure. Her belly flip-flopped in sensual delight as she noticed dampness between her legs.

"All the way. Damn, you're good." Jet's voice carried to her ears, the words bit out as if he spoke through clenched teeth. "Get down on my cock. Now."

She couldn't see his face but knew he must be getting close. He reached out, grabbed Garrett's hips, and yanked him down with a slapping sound as their bodies met.

Garrett moaned low, rocking forward and backward, Jet's strong grip keeping him from doing more than grinding against his lover, gyrating as if he couldn't get enough of Jet's presence inside his body.

"You're knotting." Garrett whimpered, then cried out, his body jerking taut.

Rain watched as his buttocks tightened, the muscles flexing beneath the white skin. He leaned forward, rested his hands on Jet's chest, and arched his back, presumably tied with Jet's swollen gland locked inside. A short volley of whitish-colored fluid caught her attention before falling out of view. Intrigued, she fought the urge to move closer, to see the expression on both men's faces, to touch the end of Garrett's cock, scoop up a drop of his release, and taste.

The risqué thoughts shook her out of her enthrallment. Without noise, she retreated the way she came, not stopping until she plopped down on the front porch steps. *What came over me, watching like that?* Astonishment at her actions only mildly reduced her lingering arousal. She'd seen couples engaged in sexual acts before. As a species, wolf shifters weren't known for a need for privacy when the desire hit. Instead, they made do with the moment at hand, not caring if prying eyes watched. Normally, if she stumbled across a pair and saw nude bodies, she'd turn right around and leave. Not today — and never before had she been turned on by simply watching a natural act. The fact rattled her already shaken state.

Doubts and confusion made her drop her face in her hands. *When did my life become so ridiculously complicated? More importantly, what in the world am I going to do?*

* * * *

Jet zipped up his jeans, noting Garrett had already dressed. Even with the addition of clothing, Garrett looked like a gorgeous gift from the gods, hunky and powerful, man enough to make Jet's mouth water with anticipation for the next time they could strip down and bring one another to a roaring climax. He'd never get enough of his mate.

*Speaking of mates...* He sniffed the air once more, a wry grin followed. Rain. "Did you happen to notice we had company a little while ago?"

Garrett's gaze met his. "I thought I heard something but was too distracted to pay much attention."

"Seems Rain came back early. I couldn't see her face but heard and smelled her."

"And?"

"She stuck around for a few minutes. Judging by her scent, I'd say she enjoyed the show."

Garrett snorted. "And you keep claiming she's innocent."

"She is. In body and in all this fiasco."

"Time will tell." Garrett shrugged and walked into the hallway.

Jet trailed behind, considering his words. At least Garrett wasn't lashing out at her as he did before. Maybe, just maybe, he'd gotten the message.

He followed his nose straight to Rain. Garrett trailed behind, choosing to remain standing and lean against one of the corner posts of the steps while Jet sat beside her.

"How did the meeting with your father go?" He searched her face and found traces of worry and fatigue. The lingering scent of her arousal hardened his groin once more. He ignored the discomfort, focusing on the present. He'd mount her soon enough when life settled down and the killer had been found—then, and only then, would he take her.

She sighed and stared at her feet. "As well as could be expected, I guess. He doesn't know anything about the murder."

"And we should believe that why?" Garrett snapped.

Rain's head jerked up. "He didn't lie. I could tell if he tried. The information shocked and upset him." She glared at Garrett another moment before turning to Jet. "He said he would call your alphas and discuss this with them."

"Good enough." Jet patted her thigh, noting the way she allowed the small gesture of comfort. "What else did he say?"

She shook her head.

He refused to be deterred. Something had upset her, and he'd bet a month's wages the responsibility lay with her alpha father. "He still doesn't accept our mating?"

"No. He said he couldn't. Not right now."

Jet processed the words carefully. "Which means there's a possibility for the future."

"I guess so."

As much as he wanted to push her for answers, Jet stayed the course, hoping Rain would volunteer her thoughts freely. When she remained silent, he grappled with his patience. Knowing she hurt made his inner wolf sit up and growl. As much as he needed to ease her pain and fretting, he needed for her to make the first step, to show some trust in him. He saw and smelled her confusion, her wariness, but didn't believe an overbearing shove would do more than clam her up all the more.

Garrett had no such qualms. "You liked watching us fuck."

"What?" Her face turned crimson.

Jet opened his mouth, but Garrett talked over him. "Don't bother to lie. We can smell your arousal."

"I just... I didn't mean..." She scrubbed her face with her hands. "I'm sorry. I didn't mean to invade your privacy."

"But you liked what you saw?" Jet asked, waiting eagerly for her answer, knowing the truth but needing her verbal admission.

"I..." She peered up at Garrett, then Jet before lowering her gaze to the steps once more. "I couldn't walk away."

Pride and hope flared inside Jet. He wrapped an arm around her and pulled her close enough to kiss her temple. "That's okay, sweetheart. Garrett and I don't mind if you watch."

He looked up and met Garrett's eyes. A small frown covered his face, but he didn't appear hostile—a definite improvement from yesterday. With any luck, a sign of things to come.

Garrett's phone rang. He quickly answered. "Yeah? No shit. When? Okay. We'll be right there."

Jet stared at Garrett, sensing the bad news to come.

"Another body. Same place."

Jet swore under his breath. "Who this time?"

"No one knows, since he's not a Spring Hill pack member." Garrett glanced over at Rain. "He's only been dead around an hour or so, according to the forensics team."

"Rain was here with us." He spoke the words Garrett must have thought.

"Yeah." Garrett didn't say anything more, but at least he acknowledged the fact.

"Let's get moving. The sooner we get the information, the sooner we can start to backtrack the killer." Jet stood up.

Rain followed. "I'm going with you."

Jet spun around and met her gaze. "It's not going to be pretty."

She nodded and swallowed. "I know."

He studied her for a long moment and decided she had as much on the line in this investigation as the rest of them—maybe even more. "Okay. Let's get moving."

Much like yesterday, they moved as a group, heading toward the dividing line between their pack lands.

\* \* \* \*

As she approached, Rain noticed a small gathering of men, Spring Hill forensics most likely. Austin stood to one side, speaking to a silver-haired man. Even as she watched, one of the men surrounding the downed body stepped to the side, allowing her a glimpse of the deceased. Her heart sped as her breathing escalated.

After hurrying over, she dropped to the man's side, stared into his scratched face, and gasped. "Oh my god."

Jet squatted beside her. "What is it?"

She tentatively reached out to touch the body then pulled her hand back. A lump formed in her throat. "It's Darin."

"Who's Darin?" Garrett asked as he lowered to one knee opposite them.

"A Horizon pack member and my friend." She looked up at Garrett. "Why would anyone do this? Everyone liked him. He always had a smile and a corny joke." She focused her attention on the torn clothing and deep gouges. "He didn't deserve this. Any of this. Why? Just tell me why?"

Garrett shook his head, his deep gray eyes stormy. "I wish I knew."

Grief and anger at the senseless slaying hit her square in the chest. She struggled to breathe and grappled with maintaining her composure.

Jet grabbed her arm, hauled her back to her feet, and dragged her several paces away from the scene. Once they were well away from any visual reminders, he spun her around and wrapped her in his embrace.

Rain resisted for only a moment before relenting, soaking up his strength as she melted into his body.

"I've got you." He rubbed her back and nuzzled her cheek.

"It's all my fault. If I had done what my father wished, those men would still be alive." Her heart broke at the basic truth.

Jet set her back slightly then lifted her chin until she met his gaze. "Listen to me. This is not your fault. None of it. You bear no responsibility for this at all."

"Then who does?"

"I don't know." He kept hold with one arm around her waist.

"I defied my father. Came here. Now two people are dead. It can't just be a coincidence, not when our packs have held a truce for close to a thousand years." The facts couldn't be denied. Everything pointed back to her. Jet might've wanted to candy-coat things, but she knew deep down that the buck stopped with her. While she hadn't delivered the death blow herself, she might as well have, since her defiance had started this whole mess. Her gut clenched as a wave of illness washed over her.

"We'll find who's responsible. I promise you." Jet spoke with confidence. "This isn't your fault."

"I wish I could believe that." She held onto him like a lifeline, taking a moment longer to lose herself in his support. Then steeling her resolve, she stood back, pushed flyaway hairs from her face then turned toward Horizon lands. Her father needed to know about this latest twist, and the terrible news might come better from her. She started toward home. Jet's voice stopped her.

"Rain? Where are you going?"

She paused to answer. "To tell Father. Darin is...was one of his favorites." With one more look at Jet's concerned face, she jogged away.

# Chapter Nine

Jet slapped the dirt off his jeans, wiped his shoes, then entered the cabin. He'd spent most of the day reassigning patrol duties, doubling up everyone for safety until the murder mystery could be solved. His brother had personally spoken to the alpha of Horizon Pack, hammering out a deal to try to keep their personnel calm, yet cognizant and cautious. With a bunch of grumbling and fretting between them, they'd finally agreed to a temporary solution of adding more guards to the borders and keeping the more vulnerable members restricted to the center areas and in their homes.

Hearing a sniffle, Jet frowned and walked forward, intent on getting to Rain and finding out what had her so upset. He paused at the threshold of her bedroom and absorbed the sight of her curled up on the bed, wiping at her puffy eyes as she tried to even out her breathing. Poor, brave Rain. He wondered when she'd finally release her pent-up emotions. All the angst and tension with the impromptu mating, her angry father, Garrett's accusing words and attitude, and now two murders in the span of twenty-four hours. Anyone would be at their breaking point by now.

"Rain?" Softly he called her name and entered the room, certain she'd sensed him when he'd arrived. He debated upon intruding on her private meltdown, but her tears were ripping his heart out. "What's wrong?"

Immediately, she sat up, sniffed once more, and used the sheet to blot at the tears streaming down her face. "Nothing."

He shook his head sadly, strode over, then took a place on the bed beside her. "We all cry now and again. It's just part of who we are."

She blinked away the last tears. "It's just a pity party."

"Who told you that?"

"Everyone knows it." She clasped her hands together and focused on them.

He nudged her with his shoulder. "Not everyone. Besides, in order for us to feel happiness and joy, we have to also experience pain and suffering. Otherwise, how would we know how lucky we are?"

Rain remained quiet, but her breathing evened out, a signal she regained control over her volatile emotions for the moment.

"Even men cry." He added in the last bit, hoping for her to understand his philosophy on grief, a belief his whole pack shared.

When the statement didn't garner a reply, he changed tactics. After pulling her against him, Jet kissed her temple. "It's okay, sweetheart. I promise we'll figure this all out."

A tear trickled down her cheek. "My father is angry, blaming Spring Hill. My friend is dead. Our packs are on the brink of all-out war—all because of me."

He kissed her nose and rubbed her back, hoping to calm and support her. "Again. Not your fault. Let the alphas work things out. We're certainly helping investigate the deaths. Everything will come to pass in the end. One day at a time."

She turned her head, looked up at him, her large eyes glistening with unshed tears, beseeching him to help ease her pain, to help her forget all the problems at hand for a few minutes. Ever so slowly she meshed her lips with his. Almost tentatively, she settled over his mouth in a chaste experiment.

Jet responded immediately, seizing control over the expression of affection, opening his mouth, flicking his tongue over her bottom lip, and encouraging her to do the same. The moment she did, his passion exploded.

Deepening the kiss, he delved into her mouth, seeking the recesses in order to taste her essence, to share his burning need with her. She responded in kind, slipping her tongue into his mouth and engaging in a quick wrestling match.

In the back of Jet's mind, his conscience dinged, a loud warning bell of sanity. He broke the contact and panted for breath.

Studying her flushed face, he asked the pressing question presently holding him back. "I know you're upset and seeking comfort. This probably isn't the best time to be together for the first time. Maybe we should wait for a better time?"

"No. Right now. I need you, Jet. Please show me. Teach me. Make me yours." The sincere words sealed her fate.

With tempered gusto, he covered her mouth once more, reacquainting himself with her individual flavor while he dipped his hand under the hem of her shirt. He traced the lines of her belly then headed north, seeking and finding her bra-clad breasts. Cupping one in his palm, he weighed the breast while stroking his thumb over the area.

Rain moaned and pressed closer. Then she caught the same fever he had. She yanked at his shirt, jerking until the material gave way then moved to the buttons on his jeans. Jet stood up, flicked the fly open, and let the material drop before stripping her down at a reckless pace. Her shirt fell to the floor, followed by her pants. Before she had a chance to step out of the small puddle of garments, he tore the bra and rent her panties into pieces.

Only when she stood naked did he regain control over his wild instincts. After stepping out of the jeans shackling his ankles, he put a couple of steps between them. First, he needed a moment to cool down and use his head instead of his rampant hormones. If he didn't collect himself and fast, he risked making a painful mess of her first time. Such a precious gift needed to be treasured and savored. Secondly, he needed to take in the sight of his newest mate in the buff, to commit the vision to memory.

Her smaller frame curved in all the right places. Raspberry nipples topped modest breasts. A trim waist led down to flared hips and slender legs, the junction between the two covered with short dark brown curls.

"Beautiful. Absolutely beautiful."

She stood still for his rapt appraisal as her gaze raked his body from head to toe, lingering an exceptionally long time on his groin. His cock jumped as she stared, awe and a bit of intimidation crossed her face. Her little pink tongue flicked out to coat her lips. He nearly groaned at the thought of her doing the same to the tip of his engorged member, licking the bead straight from his slit. She would open wide, enveloping his mushroomed head inside her mouth, where her tongue would flick over him like steamy feathers until he reached a roaring orgasm, sending jets of hot seed down her throat. The mental image revved up his already heightened libido.

Grasping his control with tight reins, he reached for her once more, softly exploring every curve as he placed small caresses along her jawline, to her earlobe, then up the column of her throat. Resisting the temptation of her ruby lips, he dipped his head and drew a peaked nipple into his mouth.

Rain gasped, even as her hands bracketed his head, holding him tight against her bosom. She moaned loudly, spurring him into action.

After picking her up in a cradle hold, he carried her to his bedroom and quickly deposited her in the center of the spacious bed. Once she laid spread out before him, he took a moment to feast on the sight until his cock began to throb with immediate need.

"Are you sure about this?" His conscience demanded that he give her one more opportunity to change her mind.

"Yes. Please. I need you, Jet." Rain reached out for him.

She'd probably carry regrets later, but he couldn't any more walk away from her right now than he could sprout wings and fly to the moon. He'd shoulder any ramifications for losing his mind in the heat of the moment if and when the need arose.

He climbed on the bed then crawled over until he straddled her body, giving himself easy access to every inch of her delectable flesh. He'd strum her to a fever pitch, ensure she was ready then sink into her softness.

Without further ado, he began the journey of a lifetime, starting with a fiery kiss, hard and hungry. Rain's hand encircled his erection, causing him to break away and sit back. He watched her face as she explored—the wonder and appreciation clear. Each tentative caress made his blood boil hotter, yet he clamped down on the urge to rush forward. Instead, he sat still as marble, letting her learn his body.

"You're so big. How does Garrett take it all?" she whispered as she measured his length with the tips of her fingers.

His cock leaped at her touch, forcing a groan from his throat. He shot her a toothy grin, the best he could do while grappling with his inner wolf demanding he take his mate right now.

"He's had a lot of practice."

"Does it hurt?"

She dipped farther south, cupping his sac and gently weighing his balls. He sucked in a breath, unable to answer for a long moment before grasping her wrist loosely and pulling her inquisitive hands away from his body.

"No more for now."

Her brow furrowed.

"I'd rather spend myself inside you than on the sheets."

"Oh."

He focused back on her previous question. "Are you asking if I hurt Garrett when we have intercourse or if I'll hurt you?" He held her gaze and waited.

"Both."

After leaning down, he kissed her again, palmed a breast, and caressed the nipple into a hard peak. "First times are somewhat difficult, no matter if you're male or female. I'll be easy, and we'll go slowly. As for

Garrett, I can't and won't hurt the man I love. He likes sex fairly rough, so I cater to his needs."

He replaced his mouth with his hand, which he rubbed across her belly, pausing at her bikini line. "Just like I'll cater to yours." He meandered lower until he covered her center. "Open for me, Rain. Show me you want this as much as I do."

Slowly, she splayed her legs, allowing him the room he needed to explore further. He sucked her breast at the same time he parted her tender lips, felt the moisture. With precision, he found her opening and slid one finger inside.

Rain gasped, her muscles tensed at the dual loving attack on her untried body. He paused only long enough to switch breasts, flicking his tongue over the tip.

He twisted his wrist and tunneled his thumb between the folds until he discovered her hooded clit. With exquisite finesse, he circled the area before barely brushing over the nub itself. Rain grasped the sheets tightly, her hips lifted as she pressed closer to his fingers.

She opened her eyes and locked onto his gaze. Sparks of passion flashed in the pretty purple-ish irises while her face contorted as if she were on a rack of intense pleasure.

Jet doubled the presence inside her body, using the generous moisture to ease his way. Spreading his fingers, he worked to loosen the snugness, to prepare her thoroughly to accept his erection.

"I need…" She bit off the words on a low whine.

"I know, sweetheart. Soon, I promise."

"Now. More. Now." She shook her head, her long brunette locks tangling as they were pulled this way and that.

"Patience. Let me stretch you a bit more so I don't hurt you when I cover you." Jet tried to soothe her while pressing her to the very limits, keeping her simmering just a notch or two below orgasm. Her enjoyment of her first time depended on his attention to details and perseverance to ensure she transitioned into full womanhood with flying colors and a healthy appetite for more.

He sawed with his fingers, pressed deeply then splayed his digits to widen the entrance. The whole time, she writhed and wiggled, her slit dampening all the more.

He clenched his teeth and pulled from her body, his control strained to the breaking point. Repositioning himself between her thighs, he sucked in a calming breath. "Rain?"

She turned her head to stare at him, her eyes half glazed with sultry need.

"Watch." He set his tip against her folds then eased forward. She welcomed him with heat and wetness and a tightness that nearly took his breath away. He stayed the course, not slowing or speeding up, simply lazily joining their bodies as if they had all day to fuse together. Her body eased before him after a stubborn initial resistance.

"Am I hurting you?" He watched every nuance of her expression, searching for the slightest indication of discomfort.

"No. It's incredible." She panted out as she spread her legs wider, giving him more than ample room to work.

Her words whipped him to greater heights then she flinched.

He understood why a second later as he butted up against a barrier blocking him from progressing further. Not unexpected in her untried state, but he had hoped she didn't possess a hymen. With the membrane intact, discomfort was unavoidable.

He slid back a couple of inches then returned, giving her a preview of what was to come.

She braced herself against the covers, clinging to the linens under her fingers as she tensed in preparation.

"Shhh." Jet stopped and stretched out over her body, resting his weight on bent elbows. His lips settled on hers, enticing her into a heated kiss. For the longest time, he simply continued the oral foray, waiting for her to relax enough to take the next giant step in their lovemaking.

Satisfied when she mewled her pleasure, he tested the waters with a slow stroke forward, met the obstacle, then pressed some more. Rain jerked under him, her face screwing up in acute pain. With a muttered curse, he shifted back and forth a few times, shallow thrusts just barely inside her until she eased once more. Gathering up his strength, he surged ahead, felt the membrane give way, and sank fully into her depths.

Rain hissed and bucked. He absorbed her brief struggle until she settled back on the mattress, her muscles taut, still grimacing.

Holding completely still, Jet found her lips, enticing her to respond to his gentle kiss and teasing nibbles. After only a few moments, she began to reciprocate, slowly at first then with more enthusiasm.

The tension gradually ebbed from her as he showered her with affection, wanting to build her excitement back to its previous level, to apologize for her pain, to show her how good he could make this for her if she'd just let him.

He eased back marginally then returned, slowly acclimating her to the feel of his cock buried within her. "Hurt?"

She shook her head and gasped as he arched his back for the deepest penetration yet. "I feel so full. So...complete."

Her words stoked his ego and lashed his arousal to a higher pitch. With care, he began thrusting at a snail's pace, his gaze focused on her expressive face. In. Out. Her hips lifted, meeting his next stroke as she whimpered.

"Yes. Just like that."

She writhed under his attentions, pressed closer to him, and finally wrapped her arms around his neck. Her short nails dug into the skin of his back as he picked up the speed and power.

The added stimulation made his cock twitch as a tingling began low in his back. His balls tightened. Delaying his own release, he strove to push Rain over the edge of fulfillment. She needed to find rapture this first time. Anything less would fall short of a successful initiation in his bed.

"That's it, baby. Grind against me. Take my cock. All of it."

He tilted to the side, resting his weight on one arm, using his now free hand to search between them until he discovered her clit. He caressed the area, felt her tighten, heard her breath catch. Again he strummed his fingers over the nub before delicately pinching.

She whimpered and threw her head back, her chest rising and falling with the effort to suck in great gulps of air.

Once more he plucked.

Rain locked for a second more before rhythmic contractions squeezed his buried shaft inside her tight and hot channel. Her face contorted in a grimace of bliss.

He growled as his pinnacle fast approached. With one final surge, he settled in deep, felt the knot swell to its peak, and sank his teeth into the junction of her neck as the first volley of semen jetted into her depths. Crashing waves of climax rolled over him, aided by Rain's lingering rapture, her muscles clamping down now and again, setting off another explosion in his primed body.

For long minutes, he rode the tide before his gland and dick began to deflate, releasing him from his tied status. Finally able to catch his breath, he peered down at Rain, halfway concerned with her silence.

She met his gaze, her eyes spoke of a woman well loved, her body relaxed under his as she lightly rubbed his back with the tips of her fingers. As he watched, her lips hitched up in a wry grin.

"Well worth waiting for."

Relief and pride filled him. He smiled wide. "I'm glad." With a quick kiss, he levered his weight back on his knees and pulled his spent cock from her body. Rain flinched and sucked in a breath. He decided she most likely grappled with soreness and the sensation of his flesh stroking over her extra sensitive slit. "There's more where that came from. Later." Tracing his fingers down her thigh, he smiled at her. "How about we take a quick shower, then I'll take you out to eat?"

"Isn't Garrett supposed to return from his patrol soon?" She chewed her bottom lip.

"Not for a while yet. There's plenty of time for us to grab some food." He hated the signs of nervousness when she spoke of Garrett. Given a bit more time, he hoped she'd relax around his mate, accept his presence with welcome arms.

She blinked at him coyly. "Wait. Aren't you supposed to wine and dine me first, then have sex?"

His grin widened. "Okay. Maybe I'm backward this time. Next time, I'll be sure to get it right."

The corners of her mouth curled up as she sat up next to him before sliding off the bed and standing. "Next time?"

He gained his feet. "Most definitely." After placing a quick kiss on her nose, he swatted her rear lightly in an effort to get her moving toward the bathroom.

She giggled and headed toward her smaller bedroom, giving Jet a remarkable view of her delectable backside. His cock twitched, blatantly pleading for more. He ignored the mild ache, reminding himself of her probable soreness and potential discomfort if he pushed her limits too far too fast.

The experience with her ranked with the best sexual escapades in his life, right alongside Garrett. However, as wondrous and beautiful as the event was, something nagged incessantly at him. Her scent never changed.

In the case of a true mating, the female would immediately go into heat during or following her first intercourse with the lucky man. Her scent would change, making the event easily detectible with a wolf shifter's advanced olfactory sense.

His only personal experience with true mating had been with Garrett. Males didn't go into heat. Instead he'd described the sensation as love at first sight. They'd clicked and hadn't been able to keep their hands off one another. Fast, furious, and at a complete frenzy that had set the sheets afire. Friendship and companionship had come later, after they'd cooled their arousal down long enough to actually talk.

Disappointment covered him like a low hanging cloud. He would have bet all his assets that Rain would be their other mate and couldn't understand why she didn't take on a sultry aroma that would drive him and his horny cock to distraction. *Maybe we just need a bit more time together?* After all, things had happened so quickly, in stressful, chaotic times. Perhaps Rain needed time to settle down, to adjust to him, to allow her life to once more stabilize before her hormones clicked in. The reasoning sounded as good as anything else to him.

No sense worrying about something he had no control over. Much better to turn his attentions elsewhere, like wooing Rain and showing her just how much he appreciated not only her once in a lifetime gift, but also prove she belonged by his side.

With renewed determination, he strode to his bathroom, turned on the shower, and stepped in.

# Chapter Ten

"This is delicious." Rain poked another spoonful of goulash into her mouth. "Not too spicy, not too bland."

Jet grinned over his glass of soda. "Told you so."

"You did." She chewed on a soft piece of pasta before taking a small bite from the slice of bread provided with the meal.

She found being with Jet more fun and relaxing than she first imagined. After all, they'd just slept together a couple of hours ago—her first time and their initial sexual experience. Yet, she didn't feel the least embarrassed or awkward, just comfortable as if she'd had lunch with an old friend. A perfect bonding except for one thing—she hadn't gone into heat immediately.

She couldn't shake the disappointment hovering over her. Somehow being labeled as a true mate would've made the whole messy situation right—at least in her mind.

"Don't look so worried. Garrett will come around."

Rain blinked, realizing Jet had picked up on her worries, yet had missed the target on the true cause. She declined to correct him. "I'm not so sure. He's very protective of you. That's good, but I'm not sure there's room in his heart for more than you."

"Do you want him to have room for you as well?" Jet tilted his head.

She puffed out a breath. "Honestly, yes. You love one another. You're mates. How could I take one without the other?"

"But?"

"There's no but. I just wish I knew how to make him see the truth." Rain pushed another piece of pasta around her plate. "It's like he's already in the mindset that I'm the enemy and will never be able to budge."

Jet took another bite of his lunch and nodded. "It seems that way right now, but he'll ease up."

"How do you know?" She met his gaze, needing to know real hope existed in Garrett relenting his vex against her.

"Let me tell you something about Garrett." Jet sipped his drink then replaced the glass on the table. "He lost his father at a very young age. Grew up with only the alpha and a couple of other men in the pack to provide male influence."

She gasped. "Packs take care of their own. Why didn't Spring Hill care for him?"

"Because he's not Spring Hill. He's Golden Branch."

Rain digested this bit of information, racking her brain for any information on the small group of wolf shifters she knew. "Limited numbers. Reclusive. Led by an aging alpha who's rumored to be a bit unstable."

"Yep. They're definitely different." He wiped his hands on the napkin. "Anyway, growing up fatherless left a mark on Garrett. He's always watching out for the orphans in the pack, even set up a mentor program — which he leads — to make sure no child will have to grow up without a positive role model in the absence of one or both parents."

*Garrett surrounded by children?* She grinned at the image. "I thought you said Spring Hill steps in for the children who lost a parent."

He nodded. "They do. Only Garrett takes everything one step further. He makes sure none of them lack for anything."

"Which explains his overprotective attitude toward you and bitterness toward me. If he's had to struggle through life, he'd make certain to hang onto those things he feels attached to, make sure they were safe, and secure, too." She now understood more about the beta and would probably be even worse if she were in his shoes.

"You got it. It's not you, per se. It's the threat you present."

She pondered the words. "I'm not sure it's that simple."

The corner of Jet's mouth hitched up. "Things rarely are."

\* \* \* \*

"Jet?" Garrett yanked the front door closed behind him, in too much of a hurry finding his mate to make certain it latched. Striding through the house, he followed his nose until he stood right outside their bedroom.

The smell of sex permeated the whole house, along with Jet's and Rain's individual scents. Bed linens were crumpled, leaving no doubt of what activity had occurred in the bed not long ago. Jet and Rain had had sex in the bed. *Their bed*. The place only Jet and Garrett had lain and played before.

Another round of jealousy and anger hit Garrett squarely in the gut. They'd waited for him to get pulled to work then most likely couldn't keep their hands off one another, the floozy luring Jet to the bedroom and having her way with him. They couldn't hold off until he could be present, couldn't bother to tell him of their plans. Just did what they wanted, and no one cared enough to let him in on the big secret.

Garrett growled and slammed his fist against the doorframe. The small sting only registered marginally compared to the branding iron currently charring his heart.

Voices carried to him from the front porch. Regaining his composure, he crossed his arms over his chest and waited for the pair to enter the living room.

Rain entered first, a radiant smile covering her face. Jet quickly followed, reaching out to wrap his arm around her waist. Then they saw him.

Jet studied him for a long moment as Rain looked at him, lowered her gaze then chewed her bottom lip.

"I take it no new bodies since you didn't call us?" Jet stepped forward, subtly placing his body between Rain's and Garrett's.

"No." Garrett spit out the word, grappling with his emotions at seeing his mate obviously so happy with the woman who'd started all this mess.

"Umm. I need to check in with my business partner. If you'll excuse me, I'll go call her." Like a shot, Rain hurried out of the front door.

Garrett watched her go then turned his attention on his alpha mate. Jet stood at the front storm door watching Rain. The heavy scent of Jet's arousal filled the room before he finally turned to meet Garrett's gaze.

"There's something fishy going on."

Garrett snorted. "Yeah. I'd say so. Claiming Rain in our bed without the decency of at least telling me." He crossed his arms over his chest and glared.

Jet's mouth opened then shut once more before he sighed. "It was a heat of the moment thing. I didn't plan on it." He stepped closer. "Surely you expected me to take her at some point?"

"Since you can't keep your eyes off her, I guess so." Garrett shrugged, ignoring the flaring green monster prodding him.

Running his fingers through his coal black hair, Jet puffed out a breath. "Rain is something special."

"If you say so."

"Why can't you see past the atypical mating declaration?"

"Why can't you think with your head instead of your dick? Rain drew you into this, now a pack member is dead. How can you believe there's no blood on her hands?"

"Because there's not. She's a tool in some sick game, as much as you and I are." Jet's voice held conviction.

"I wished I believed you." Garrett turned away.

Jet grabbed his arm and spun him back around. "Why *can't* you believe me? You've trusted me on everything before. Now, you're calling me three kinds of fool to my face." His grip tightened marginally. "Don't give me crap about Rain taking your place in my life or my bed. We both know that's not going to happen. So cut to the chase and spit it out."

"Things are out of my control. You make decisions without consulting me. It's pissing me off and smacks of a blatant challenge." There, he said it. The whole issue boiled down to being cut from Jet's personal life when matters involved Rain. His inner wolf chafed at having no chance for an opinion, a protest, or even the tiniest opportunity to vent how he felt. No one made decisions for him, hadn't since he reached puberty. His wolf demanded respect, a fair shake, and stewardship over his own life. Jet tried to take that away. For that, he couldn't forgive him or tolerate any more infractions without complications between his wolf nature and his actual behavior.

Jet blinked. "I'll admit I screwed up. Once. I promised to never do so again and haven't."

"You fucked her on our bed. Where the hell was I?" Garrett crossed his arms over his chest and growled low in his throat.

Jet's dark eyes flashed. "You just said this isn't about Rain. It's about me—and you." He slowly bobbed his head. "It's your nature. Your alpha nature." The soft words carried easily.

Garrett's mouth fell open. He kept that part of himself in check, comfortable with his beta status until recently. Now, his wolf barraged him with demands, orders, and willfulness to step up and make sure his mate toed the line.

He'd never even heard of two alphas mating, probably due to the inevitable conflicts that were bound to arise. Since he'd accepted a lesser status most of his life, remaining a beta had never posed an issue until Rain showed up and Jet started flexing his alpha muscle.

"That's it, isn't it?" Jet ran one hand through his short hair. "I noticed it the other day. You didn't avert your gaze. Deep down, you're as alpha as I am." He made the statement calmly, without accusation.

"I don't know and don't intend to find out." Garrett scowled.

"You can't keep playing a role at being something you're not," Jet advised.

"I can when our relationship depends upon it." He'd been doing that very thing since they became mates several years ago. It hadn't been an issue until now.

Garrett stared at the man he loved for a moment more before pushing past him to head out of the door. Maybe after a long run in the woods, he'd manage to cool down and temper his rage. If anyone believed that, he had some swampland for sale in the high desert.

# Chapter Eleven

Unwilling to return to the fire pit otherwise known as Jet and Garrett's house, Rain wandered toward the center of the pack community area, noting several children playing. Adults stood around or sat at picnic benches, obviously monitoring the kids, reminding her of her childhood. Her mother had watched her like a hawk, ensuring trouble never even tempted her—probably the reason she'd snuck out and rebelled when she could. Too strict, too many rules, not enough room to flex her independence and become her own person. Horizon Pack was uptight and stifling. Definitely a contrast with Spring Hill, which in her limited experience appeared much more accepting and laid back—a great place to grow up.

Nearby, she noted a small girl, probably around three or four years old, futilely trying to tag along with her brother, who darted off with a group of boys, ball in hand. The little brunette tried her best but finally tripped, landing hard on her bottom.

Even with all the parents around, Rain couldn't stop herself from going to the youngster. She moved in slowly the last few steps then knelt to be at eye level with the child. "Hi there."

The girl's large brown eyes locked with hers.

"Are you okay?"

The girl sniffled. "Bubba..."

Reaching out, Rain offered her arms. The girl mimicked the gesture until Rain picked her up, resting her naturally on her hip. She wiped a single tear away. "Boys are ornery. But I'll tell you a secret."

The girl stared at her intently.

"Girls have much more fun than they do. All boys do is roll around in the dirt and chase after balls, even wrestle. We get to play on the jungle gym, share secrets, and make flower necklaces."

"Flower?"

"Yep. Flower necklaces. I'll be glad to show you how."

"Okay."

The girl found the ribbon in Rain's hair and tugged, loosening the bow. With a gentle yank, she pulled her new treasure to her chest.

Rain smiled and rubbed her nose against the child's. "My name's Rain. What's yours?"

"Beth."

"Well, Beth, how about you and I find some flowers to make into necklaces, and I'll put the ribbon in your hair?"

For the first time, Beth grinned. "Okay." She wiggled to be put down.

As soon as Rain set her on her feet, the girl grabbed her hand and began leading her toward a patch of blooming dandelions. "Hurry."

"I'm coming." Rain felt someone watching her. Glancing up, she found Garrett standing to the side of the clearing, his gaze on her while his expression appeared perplexed.

Beth pulled once more. "Come on."

Shooting Garrett a lopsided smile, Rain followed along after her new friend.

Garrett sucked in a breath, watching Rain being led off by the small girl. He'd seen the child fall and started for her until he saw Rain reach her. He couldn't hear their conversation, but he easily read both their faces. Rain relaxed and seemed to actually enjoy the child while Beth's tears dried up immediately when Rain started talking. Judging by the beaming smile, Beth had found a new playmate and had forgotten all about chasing after her older brother.

*She'd make a good mother.*

The moment the words popped into his mind, he realized they were simply the truth. Her interaction with Beth showed him a couple of things. First, she appeared to be a natural with kids. Second, doubts about her accountability for the deaths and escalating tension between their packs leaked through his formerly solid beliefs. An underhanded killer and manipulator wouldn't take the time to dry a child's tears and put a smile back on her face, not in a brand-new pack that she would have plotted against. Sure, she could be an excellent actress, but she couldn't pull off the genuine pleasure and comfort as soon as she picked up the child and held her tightly, yet gently. She seemed to truly care for the girl's predicament and step up to make things right in Beth's world.

For the first time, he saw her as something other than the villain in the lamentable play they'd all been acting out.

Maybe, just maybe, Rain was something other than he'd first believed.

With one more look at Rain sitting in the grass plucking dandelions with Beth, Garrett spun on his heel and headed back to the perimeter section he'd recently vacated. After the rollercoaster ride of earlier, he needed space and time to think. Might as well check out and protect the borders while he did so.

\* \* \* \*

Garrett strode toward the peak of a nearby hill, kicking at a rock now and again along the way. The vantage point from there allowed him to oversee several acres by simply turning around. Most of the land proved flat, but this small rise stood out as the exception, a good one at that. Even with the dim light of sunset, he could easily make out trees, rocks, and an occasional wild animal as they lumbered around searching for their evening meal.

No sooner had he reached the top than a scuffling sound caught his attention. Turning this way and that, he located the direction and sprinted off, his heart sinking at the possibility of arriving too late. He skidded down a steep slope, hurdled a downed log then ripped through a scattering of trees before nearly trampling the body lying on the ground. Someone crashed through the brush just ahead. As much as Garrett wanted to pursue, his first priority remained with the victim. Care for him, get some help, then he could hunt his quarry.

After kneeling down, he checked for a pulse and exhaled in relief. Though bloody and unconscious, the man was still alive. He checked for major wounds and found nothing life-threatening, only a knot on the man's head and some long scratches, which might scar but should otherwise heal without difficulty.

Garrett plucked his phone out and called for backup, knowing help would arrive in a few minutes. Disconnecting, he surveyed the area, knowing the culprit had to be close. He inhaled deeply and froze. The scent covering the man was familiar. Way too familiar.

"Garrett?"

Spinning at the sound of his name, Garrett found a small party of rescue personnel approaching. "He's over here."

Quickly, they skirted the jagged rocks and made their way to the injured shifter.

Garrett made a hasty decision. "Thomas? I'm going to track the perpetrator."

The highest ranking member of the small team frowned. "Shouldn't you wait for backup? Obviously this guy's dangerous."

"No time." Without another word, Garrett shifted to his wolf form and followed his nose. Every second counted, thus he used his magic to discard his clothing. Normally, he'd have been more careful, but he could afford to lose a few articles of clothing in an emergency, which this happened to be.

Running full out, he found the scent becoming fresher and more potent the closer he came. A couple of miles flew by as he focused on catching up with the suspect through forest and rough terrain before hitting a tiny gravel road. Panting hard, he zeroed in on his target only to see a flash of brake lights before an engine roared to life. The driver floored the gas, sent a wave of gravel pelting through the air, then disappeared at dangerous speeds down the back road.

Garrett stopped, his long tongue hanging out as he tried to catch his breath after the distance run. He cursed his bad luck, but didn't beat himself up over the near capture. Instead, he watched the vehicle disappear as a fiery rage boiled in his gut.

*You can run, you bastard, but you can't hide.*

With a grunt of disgust, he spun on his heel and jogged toward home.

Sure, he should call Jet, update him on the latest find. However, he chose not to. Not because of his frustration with Jet over Rain, but because he knew his mate would try to stop him or at least demand to tag along. The alpha's presence would only complicate matters. No. He needed to do this alone. His pack. His problem.

Ten minutes later, he pulled his truck out of the parking space and headed west—toward Golden Branch Pack lands.

\* \* \* \*

After rapping on the door, Garrett waited impatiently for someone to answer. Luckily, he didn't have to wait long before Denise answered.

"Garrett. This is a surprise." She smiled at him warmly. He'd liked his cousin's choice of mate and truly hoped she wasn't involved in her husband's nefarious scheme.

He wished he could've returned her enthusiasm. "Is Sawyer here?"

She blinked at him then frowned, her eyes filling with worry. "Is something wrong?"

"I just need to talk to Sawyer." He refused to drag her into this mess. If she was innocent, she didn't need him dumping such traumatic news at her feet. If she shared responsibility, he didn't want to spook her into sounding the alarm.

"Garrett. It's a bit late for a social visit, isn't it?" A tall, lanky man stepped into view behind his wife, his sandy brown hair damp, as if he'd just come from the shower.

"This is business." Garrett strode inside without an invitation. He glanced down at the short redhead. "Denise, would you excuse us for a moment? We have some pack business to discuss."

Her mouth thinned. "I don't know what this is about, but I'll find out eventually." She huffed and marched toward the back of the house.

Garrett nodded. She'd learn about the whole ordeal—just not from him and not tonight. As soon as he heard the door click behind her, he turned his attention on Sawyer.

"We need to talk."

"Yeah, I got that." Sawyer crossed his arms over his chest and stared up at Garrett. "So start talking."

"Want to explain what you were doing on Spring Hill territory tonight?"

"Why would I be there?"

The man's stoic expression didn't fool Garrett. He could smell a lie, and Sawyer knew it. From an early age, Golden Branch shifters were taught to answer questions with another question in order to evade being caught in a trap of their own making.

"You tell me."

"Did you have a point in coming here tonight besides playing games?"

Tired of the circling, Garrett opted for the direct approach. "You're responsible for the deaths of both a Spring Hill and a Horizon pack member and a brutal attack on another who was lucky enough to survive."

Sawyer opened his mouth, but Garrett spoke over him. "Don't bother to lie. We both know I can detect any untruth easily." When Sawyer said nothing, Garrett continued, "I caught your scent tonight, followed you to your truck, and saw you drive off. You killed two men and badly injured a third. Now, I want to know why."

"I have nothing to say to you." Sawyer snarled, his lip lifting to show one long fang.

Garrett's inner beast bristled at the challenge. He growled low in his throat. "You've already shown your stupidity by killing on my pack lands. Don't become an imbecile by daring to challenge me." He balled his fists and stared his cousin down.

Sawyer stepped back, a tiny sign of hesitant submission. Minimal progress.

"Why were you there? Did you cook up this plan yourself? What do you have to gain?" Each word clipped out between Garrett's still bared canine teeth.

"This isn't my fault." Sawyer began to pace back and forth across the living room floor. "Don't blame this on me."

Garrett watched him carefully, realizing he spoke the truth. While he might be responsible for killing men, Sawyer didn't feel he should be blamed for his actions. Something deeper and more sinister had to be going on.

"Who ordered the attacks?"

Sawyer froze as his face lost all color. His lips pinched together tightly as if physically sealing in the answer.

Garrett watched him for a long moment before moving into Sawyer's personal space, grabbing him by the throat and began to squeeze. Sawyer's frightened gaze met his.

"Listen to me and listen good. Your actions have nearly brought two packs into a declaration of outright war. I intend to make sure you're judged and condemned for your part in this crime. Spilling the beans is your only salvation from my tearing your throat out right this minute."

"I...can't," Sawyer choked out.

"Why not?" Garrett relaxed his hold just enough to allow the man to suck in a breath of air.

"He'll kill me."

"So will I." Garrett leaned closer and gave Sawyer a small shake. The man grabbed onto his wrist, trying to break his hold or at least, gain a chance to lessen the powerful crushing of his windpipe — useless against Garrett's superior strength and determination born of fury.

"He ordered me."

"Who's he?"

Sawyer met his gaze unflinchingly. "*He* ordered me."

The repeated words finally sunk through Garrett's hazy brain. With a final growl, he flung Sawyer aside and stormed from the house before he tore his cousin apart.

His cousin didn't deserve such a brutal death. After all, he was only following a direct command from the only person who could order such a violent action and expect Sawyer to follow through, no questions asked.

His alpha.

The truth rocked Garrett to his core. *It couldn't be.* Yet, the more he thought about the whole scenario, the more puzzle pieces clicked into place. If Horizon and Spring Hill battled and wiped one another off the map, who would benefit? Golden Branch.

Garrett's shoulders sank with the realization of his own part in the fiasco. He had told Gregori everything, let the alpha fuel the case against Rain, and had continued to feed pack secrets back to Gregori. He carried as much blame as Gregori or Sawyer. The fact he didn't know made for a piss poor excuse.

There was only one thing left to do. Come clean to his mate and confront the mastermind in his own lair.

After sliding into the driver's seat of his truck, Garrett paused for a moment then pulled out his phone. He hit the top name on his contact list and waited for the call to be answered.

"Garrett? Where are you?" Concern laced Jet's voice.

Garrett sighed and rested his free hand on the steering wheel. "I'm at Golden Branch."

"Why?"

"I know who's responsible. At least I think I do."

"What do you mean?"

"I came across the injured sentinel tonight. Arrived in enough time to stop another murder. A familiar scent covered him. Someone I knew from Golden Branch."

"Who?"

"Sawyer. My cousin."

"Oh, shit."

He heard Jet muttering to Rain and her gasping in the background. His gut clenched with shame at the thought of what he put Rain through, his dastardly treatment of the woman who tried hard to be friends. "Tell Rain I'm sorry. I was an ass to her, and she didn't deserve any of it."

"Come home and tell her yourself."

"I will. After I do something first."

"Like what?" Jet's tone took on a note of suspicion.

"Like confront Gregori."

"Hell no."

"I have to. My pack, my problem." Garrett lifted his head and stared through the windshield. "I have to do this. To prevent any more deaths...to stop a war happening."

"Damn it, Garrett. Wait for us. We'll meet you there. We can confront him together."

As much as he wanted Jet by his side, he couldn't take such a chance. Gregori hadn't held supreme alpha position over the pack for several centuries without learning a few survival skills. He'd use Rain and Jet against Garrett in a heartbeat. No way would he risk either of them.

"No time. If Sawyer doesn't go running to him with his tail tucked between his legs, I'll be surprised. Barring that, Gregori isn't dumb enough to stick around if he thinks his ruse is up." Through the phone, he heard a couple of doors slam and an engine cranking over. Jet and Rain were on the way. He had a good twenty minutes before they arrived. Perhaps a bit less if Jet drove like a maniac. "Just be sure to tell Rain I'm sorry." A lump formed in his throat. "I apologize to you as well. I just about destroyed our matehood with my stupid jealousy and accusations."

"We've worked everything out. There's nothing to forgive. Just wait for us. We're on the way."

Garrett puffed out a breath. "I love you, Jet."

"Garrett!"

He clicked off the phone before his mate could lecture him further.

Taking a moment, he focused on the task at hand. Confront his alpha. Find proof of his guilt. Then serve up judgment and sentence in one fell swoop. His conscience and duty demanded the action, even if he forfeited his life in the process.

# Chapter Twelve

"Welcome, my son." Gregori stuck out his hand. "It's been so long."

Garrett shook hands and tilted his head in bafflement. The man's scent had evolved. Now a tiny vinegar aroma emerged from him, an unpleasant odor that clung to Garrett's nostrils and made his inner wolf growl in aggression. Something had changed in the years he'd been gone—and not for the better.

"I saw Tristan outside. She's grown up fast and turned into a beautiful woman."

Gregori snapped his head around like he'd been struck. "Keep your hands off my daughter. She's not for you." An awkward tension filled the air.

Garrett stared at the alpha in shock. "I only made an observation. Trust me, I have enough mates on my hands and don't need another."

"See to it that you don't." Gregori sneered, lifting a lip to show a long fang. "Tainted blood isn't welcome."

Shoving his hands into his pocket, Garrett appeared to be taking a submissive stance but took the opportunity peek at his phone and hit Jet's cell phone number with his thumb, hoping his mate would hear the upcoming conversation. With the new stench and his alpha's erratic behavior, Garrett decided someone else besides him needed to hear what the man said. He stuck with his instincts and broached the subject he'd come to speak about.

"Have you heard anything else on the situation with Spring Hill and Horizon?"

Gregori met his gaze. "No. All I know is what I heard from you. No other members of the pack are aligned with the two involved parties." He stepped across the room to his glass of amber liquid and took a long swallow. "I haven't heard a whisper of any discourse except from you. I'll give both packs credit for knowing how to keep a secret."

"What was Sawyer doing at the scene?"

The alpha snapped his head toward Garrett. "Why would he have been there? I'm certain you're mistaken." Absently, he waved his hand.

Garrett clung to the facts. "I saw him there, leaving the scene of a gravely injured victim. His scent covered the man."

"Then he must have acted alone and in an effort to find out more about the killings. For that I shall speak to him."

After setting the drinking vessel aside, Gregori strode over to slap Garrett on the back. "You're a good son—keeping me apprised of the events, protecting your pack by bringing me information. I'm sure Sawyer was only investigating the murders in order to increase security and preparedness from your female and her devious wiles."

The words no longer stroked Garrett's pride. Instead, they whittled away at his confidence, pressed down on his moral integrity as if he'd done something terrible. "Guilt isn't proven yet."

The old alpha waved his hand. "You have proof enough with the notes left behind. Combine that with the stupid chit's status and snubbing her nose at her father. The evidence is right before your eyes."

His gut clenched as the blinders were finally lifted. *Right before my eyes.* Garrett stared at Gregori, as the fuzzy picture finally cleared up. He wanted to discard Sawyer's testimony, to believe in the man who raised him like a father. Yet, the final evidence painted the alpha's hands bright red with guilt.

"You. You're behind all this."

"How dare you accuse me?" Gregori's voice increased in decibels.

More certain, Garrett chose his words carefully. "I never told you about the note. You already said I'm your sole source of information and you'd heard nothing through the grapevine. How would you know about the note if you hadn't ordered or done the deed yourself?"

"This is our chance to rule the entire region. To rise up, claim the power, and be in total control. Let Horizon and Spring Hill kill one another off, do our dirty work. When they finish, we'll wipe out the remainders, then take our entitled throne."

"You'd let hundreds of shifters die in order to seize two thousand acres?" Garrett snarled in disgust. "What happened to you? You used to care about others. Used to be a great man."

Gregori growled low in his throat. "Used to? You fucking whelp. I'm the same man as I've always been. You're the one who's turned yellow and committed mutiny. Are the Spring Hill alphas so idiotic to allow outright challenges from their members?"

"They don't have challenges because they actually give a damn about more than sacrificing hundreds of lives for a scrap of land." Garrett showed his fangs and threw his arms up in the air. Realization and regret hit him like a hammer. All this time he'd blamed others, especially Rain, when he'd shouldered much of the responsibility as an accomplice, although unintended, for the true mastermind behind the deadly plot.

"I always knew you were going to be useful to me one day. Why else do you think I spent so much time pampering you, grooming you for a leadership position? It's paid off. Finally, Horizon and Spring Hill are at one another's throats, and I'm standing here waiting to pick up the pieces. A lifetime I've waited for just this very opportunity. You're the instrument I needed to make it happen."

"I'm the stupid one. Fucking clueless. Blamed others when you were responsible all along, encouraging me to believe all your crap, prodding me to report everything back to you. Meanwhile you sat all high and mighty, laughing as you used me and others as your pawns."

"That's right. A subservient pawn. You forget your place in questioning my wishes." Gregori stepped closer, his hands fisting so tightly that his knuckles whitened. "I'm afraid you've outlived your usefulness. Too bad. Betas are a dime a dozen and dumber than shit." He grinned wickedly. "After I finish you, I'll personally take out your mates. The alpha will know torture before he finally dies. The girl? She might provide some fun before I tear out her throat."

"No one threatens my mates."

"I just did, you bastard, low-life beta."

"Goes to show what you know. I'm an alpha."

"Bullshit. You wish you had enough balls to step into an alpha role."

"We'll see about that."

In a flash, Garrett dropped his clothes to the floor as he shifted to his wolf form. No sooner had he freed himself from the restrictive clothing than Gregori launched himself, also in canine form, crashing into Garrett's shoulder and sending him tumbling. Garrett quickly righted himself, side-stepped another attack, then circled around to nip at Gregori's hind leg, missing by a fraction. The light-colored wolf easily outweighed him by fifty pounds and stood a few inches taller, but size didn't always matter in a battle to the death. Speed, power, and ingenuity played important parts. In those, Garrett could excel.

Garrett lunged, clamped down on Gregori's ear, and held on until the appendage tore, spraying blood over the floor and onto the coats of both wolves.

With a howl of rage, Gregori charged head on.

Jumping to the side, Garrett barely cleared the vicious teeth aimed at his throat, only to find his hind leg caught. He yelped as Gregori first tore the muscle then went deeper, snapping the bone underneath.

In adrenaline-laced desperation, Garrett threw himself at the bigger wolf, toppled him, and earned his release. His claws skidded on the slippery hardwood floor now covered in bright red blood. After digging for purchase, he found his balance on three legs.

Gregori stalked him, slowly, methodically.

Garrett backed up, frantically searching for a way around, anything to seize the upper hand. Finding nothing, he lowered his head and bared his teeth, prepared to do as much damage as possible in one final flurry of activity and energy.

Gregori leaped.

Garrett countered, taking a steeper angle into Gregori's windpipe and clamped tight. No matter how much the bigger wolf shook and scratched at him with sharp nails, Garrett refused to relent.

Agony soared through him as Gregori dug his back claws into Garrett's already injured leg. He pushed the pain aside and focused on his hold, unable to generate enough traction and strength to rip the tissues. Yet, he made sure the old alpha drew no air. Time slowed to a near standstill as Garrett absorbed more punishment before Gregori showed the slightest signs of oxygen deprivation.

The light-colored wolf staggered, regained his feet then went down again with a whine.

Garrett steeled his resolve, gathered his remaining energy, and sank his teeth further. Minutes passed while he stared down at the other wolf and waited. Finally, Gregori's sides no longer rose and fell, and Garrett no longer detected a heartbeat. Only then did he release the deadly grip on Gregori's throat.

"Garrett? *Garrett!*"

Dizzy and extremely weak, Garrett collapsed just as Jet and Rain rushed to his side. He stared at the two faces, which began to fuzzily mesh into one. Lightly, he licked Rain's hand as she stroked his blood-stained fur, then the world went black.

* * * *

"Hold pressure on that artery. Tight. I'm going to floor it until we get back to Spring Hill." Jet slammed the passenger side door shut on the SUV, climbed into the driver's seat, and cranked the engine. Once he hit the road, he punched the gas, and lifted his phone to his ear.

"Austin. I need the healer. Now. Garrett. He's barely hanging on. We're on our way as fast as this son of a bitch car will go."

Rain changed hands, clamping down strong on the still oozing wound high up on Garrett's rear leg. No matter how much pressure she applied, drops of blood seeped out to stain her clothes and the vehicle's carpet. She constantly watched Garrett's side, hoping for each breath to continue until they met the healer.

Tears pooled in her eyes as she recalled the conversation both she and Jet overheard, thanks to Garrett's quick thinking. Not only had he figured out the convoluted puzzle, he'd thrown the truth in his alpha's face, stood up for his mates, and risked his life to end the threat then and there. A wolf shifter couldn't have been any braver than the sandy blond-colored wolf before her.

After all the turbulence she'd caused, she understood Garrett's animosity toward her and only wished for another chance to start over again. She'd chosen not only Jet for a mate but Garrett as well.

"Please don't die. I know you hate me, don't trust me. That's okay. I love you like I love Jet. But if you just hang on, I'll leave. You can have Jet all to yourself, anything you want, if you just promise to keep fighting, to survive this."

A tear dropped from her cheek onto the fur of his ruff. She carefully supported his injured leg and sucked in a breath. "Stay with us. We'll meet the healer in a couple of minutes. You just have to hang in there. Please. Do it for Jet—for your future together."

A lump formed in her throat, blocking any more words. She held on for dear life and prayed like she'd never prayed before.

# Chapter Thirteen

"You can see him now." The silver-haired healer gestured toward the door to his small clinic. "He's weak and won't be ready to go home for another day or so. He's been asking for you, so I see no reason why you can't have a short visit."

"Thank you." Jet stepped forward, pausing when Rain remained steadfast, despite his tug on her arm. "He'll want to see you, too."

Rain shook her head. "I don't think so." After everything they'd been through, the last thing Garrett needed was a reminder of the chaos she'd dropped into their lives. He needed rest, peace, and soothing quiet. Not another round of arguing and hostilities.

"He asked for you *both*," the healer interjected before walking off.

"See? Come on." Jet opened the door, ushered Rain in before him then stepped into the room.

Rain let her eyes adjust from the bright sunshine outside to the dimmer light inside. She let her nose lead the way to a side room. Balking, she waited for Jet to make the first move.

He moved around her, stuck his head in the door, and grinned widely. "Damn. You're all naked, and I can't do a thing about it."

Garrett snorted. "Randy as a warthog."

Jet chuckled. "Always."

Upon peeking around Jet, Rain glimpsed the injured wolf shifter, noticing his bare chest still holding pink stripes, testament to his rapid healing after the battle to the death with his former alpha.

He met her gaze and gestured to her. "Come in. Please."

Tentatively, she trailed Jet until they both stood beside the wide bed.

"Now, sit."

Jet's eyebrow shot up, but he grinned. "Seems you're wearing the alpha skin much more comfortably now."

Rain sat down, careful not to jostle the mattress and cause Garrett more discomfort.

Garrett rolled his eyes. "I'm still the same person I was before."

"But with attitude."

"Like I didn't have that before."

Jet leaned in and kissed him on the lips, a fleeting show of affection. "True." Worry crossed his face. "Speaking of alpha...you're now in charge of Golden Branch."

"No way." Garrett shook his head. "Let someone else have it. I'm not the least bit interested in stepping up as supreme leader. Not in this lifetime."

"You sure? I hear reigning has its perks."

"Positive."

Relief washed over Rain upon hearing Garrett's words. Since he'd defeated his old alpha, by rights, Garrett could step into the man's position, forcing him to change packs once again, causing further upheaval than they'd already experienced. Not a welcome thought at the moment.

"How are you feeling?" Rain asked.

His charcoal eyes met hers. "Like a damned fool."

She tilted her head in question. "There's nothing to be ashamed about. You figured out what your old alpha was doing, confronted him, and took him out. Why would that be foolish?"

Garrett reached out and grasped her hand gently in his. "I treated you like shit, refused to believe what Jet said and what I could see with my own eyes. I'm sorry."

His words cascaded over Rain like a soothing mist on a hot summer's day. She grinned at him and squeezed his hand. "All's forgiven. I would've been just as upset if I were in your shoes after barging into your happy life, pitting you against me over Jet. I would probably have been even worse."

"I doubt anyone could have been worse."

The grumbling, self-reproachful tone spurred her. Upon leaning in, she kissed his cheek. "Apology accepted. Let's leave the past where it is and move forward from here."

Jet searched her face. "Have you decided to stay?"

Put on the spot, Rain squirmed. She'd decided to return to her shop and home among the humans, leaving the men behind to carry on as they had before, releasing them from their promise — until today. When Garrett had lain barely alive in the back of the vehicle as she fought to stem the tide of blood, she'd realized they'd grown on her, despite the tenuous start. In all honestly, she preferred to stay, live with her own kind, explore what being a mate truly meant. However, more than her wishes came into consideration.

Looking up, she found both men staring at her in anticipation. "I… I'm not sure."

"What will it take to convince you to stay with us?" Jet asked.

"Are you sure that's what you both want? I'd thought to return home, to give you both your freedom back." She bit her lip as she waited their response.

"I want you here. With us," Jet answered with confidence.

She turned to Garrett and waited with bated breath.

"Stay. With us. I know I've been a prick, but I want to make up for all the pain I've caused." Garrett sucked in air.

"I don't want to stay as a balm to your pride." She had to make everything clear. Vagueness now would only lead to more conflict in the future, something she'd had more than her fill of lately.

He met her gaze as a slow smile appeared. "Stay and get to know the real me. I've been told I'm quite the charmer and ladies' man."

Jet covered his laugh with a cough. "I'll give you the charmer part. Ladies' man?" His eyebrow hitched up.

Garrett grinned all the wider. "You're spoiled. Give me a week and ask Rain if I'm not sweet as molasses."

"Providing I'm here in a week?" She couldn't resist adding some levity to the situation. Both men probably could be taken down a notch.

"Will you be?" Garrett asked.

She didn't have the heart to torment them further with waiting. "Yes. I'll be here. For as long as you both want me." The words felt right.

"For a lifetime," both men said at the same time.

\* \* \* \*

"He needs his rest. Go on home. You can come back tomorrow. Maybe take him home if he actually does what he's supposed to do." The silver-haired man glared at Garrett.

"He's worse than an old mother hen." Garrett complained and rolled his eyes at the old healer who supervised their second visit of the day.

Jet laughed. "Possibly, but without him we'd be up shit creek." Garrett looked much better now than earlier. He had more color and seemed to have made huge bounds in his recovery in a couple of short hours.

Rain patted Garrett's hand and kissed his cheek. "At least you're better. I'm so thankful for that blessing."

Garrett's gaze softened as he looked at her. "Thanks for the lasagna. It's delicious. I'll eat more later."

Jet noticed and grinned to himself. Those two were smitten. Finally. He couldn't wait for Garrett to be back up on his feet and they could find time to be together—physically. Until then, he'd happily take just being in one another's presence and bantering.

He also couldn't have been more proud of Rain, who'd hurried home earlier and had gone straight to the kitchen, making two large meat and pasta dishes for both Czar, the healer, and for Garrett. Just another example of her care and innate goodness.

Rain smiled down at Garrett, stood up, and exited behind the healer, giving Jet and Garrett a couple of moments of privacy.

"I still don't think I'll get over that scare for years to come." Jet wrapped an arm carefully around Garrett and hugged him. "I don't want to even think about living without you." A lump lodged in his throat at the unacceptable thought.

Garrett nuzzled Jet's neck and licked. "No worries on that. I don't plan for this to happen again. Besides, being a beta is a damn sight safer than this alpha shit."

Jet sat back and chuckled, thoroughly enjoying the teasing, just like the old days. He'd missed this part of their relationship immensely. "You could be right." Looking at the doorway, he sighed with resignation. "I guess I should be going before old Czar kicks me out and forbids me to return."

Garrett grabbed Jet's hand and held on tightly. "I'm coming home tomorrow. No matter what."

"I hope so, but we'll let the expert make the decision. I won't jeopardize your health or healing because I'm selfish and want you back in bed."

Garrett grinned ruefully, his eyes twinkling. "Guess that means you miss me, huh?"

"More than you know," Jet admitted.

Garrett turned sober once more. "Rain needs some attention. I can smell the upset and arousal on her."

Jet had noticed the same scent more than once. But, with Garrett's life in question and briefing his brother on what happened, Jet didn't have the time or the opportunity to do more than recognize the smell.

"See to her needs, Jet. She longs for closeness right now." Garrett's gaze pinned Jet.

Jet shook his head. "She'll balk. We both will. Not until you're back up to par and we can all share the experience together." Memories of Garrett's hurt when Jet had taken Rain for the first time without even broaching the subject with Garrett first, fired through Jet's mind.

Garrett met his gaze steadily. "I'm over that. She needs you right now. I'll catch up when I'm able."

Jet stared at his first mate, needing to be absolutely sure about such a sensitive topic. "I'm not sure."

"Damn stubborn jackass." Garrett threw up his hands. "Quit being such a mule. Take care of Rain. Fuck her, sleep with her. Hold her. Whatever she needs. She's been through a hell of a lot and it's not fair to just leave her hanging in the wind because you're afraid of stepping on my feelings." He drew in a breath. "I promise...I'm okay with this. Just help her first. Tomorrow, when I get home, we'll figure the rest out."

Jet's heart lifted at Garrett's orders. For the first time since Rain had appeared in their collective lives, he sensed no jealousy on Garrett's part. Just concern, caring, and perhaps the beginning of something deeper. He smiled, bent down, and kissed Garrett with feeling.

Before either of them could get carried away, he trailed his fingers over Garrett's cheek then reluctantly left the room.

He found Rain waiting just outside of the building, staring out across the open space, as if lost in her own thoughts. Her beauty stood out against the darker shadows like a sparkling amethyst against a dusty ground.

"Ready to go home?"

"Yeah." She smiled at him shyly and offered her hand, which he took in his.

Jet led Rain back to their cabin, a sense of relief and hope firmly lodged in his chest. Garrett would come home the next morning, needing only more time to get back on his feet, good as new. Rain had agreed to stay and Garrett had finally accepted her as their third. With the ones responsible for the two deaths and nearly all out warfare dealt with, life could return to normal. Better than normal. Joyfully full and fun.

"I can't believe Garrett took out his old alpha. That's the bravest thing I've ever heard of." Rain sighed and glanced up at Jet. "Do you think all the drama is over now?"

"I sure hope so. Nerves are still taut and I'm sure it's a wait and see between the two packs, but I think things will settle back down to normal soon enough."

"I hope Garrett doesn't regret saying he wants me to stay."

Jet snapped his head around. "Why would you say that?"

She walked a few more steps in silence. "I'm not perfect. Carry a lot of flaws, am headstrong, stubborn, and can be downright difficult."

The corners of his mouth curled up in a grin. "So can every other wolf shifter in the region."

She frowned.

He squeezed her hand before bringing hers up to brush his lips across. "Trust me. We're far from perfect as well, which, in my opinion, makes us all suited just fine."

"You're sure?" She watched him closely.

"Positive."

He'd gone over every bit of this conversation already in his head. He refused to sweat the small stuff and Garrett's vow to stick around and enjoy his two mates ceased any and all worries in Jet's mind. For the first time since the fiasco started, tension ebbed and he found himself relaxed and eagerly looking forward to the future.

He glanced at Rain as they approached the house. She worried her bottom lip, yet couldn't have been more beautiful. Her long dark hair blew lightly in the breeze, while she moved with natural grace. Her scent, unchanged still, called to him and notched his libido to high levels. He wanted her. Had since their first time together. Even before.

Today, he'd have her. Again.

"Still worried?" He tried to analyze her non-verbal clues, needing to appease her needs, settle any doubts, and reassure her she'd found a lifetime home with them.

She shook her head. "Not really. Everything feels right. Garrett is on the mend and wants to make amends." She sighed. "My father even called earlier, inviting all of us to visit anytime."

Jet arched an eyebrow at her declaration. "That's a one hundred and eighty degree turn."

"I thought so, too. When I asked, he said anyone that would challenge and kill a deranged supreme alpha responsible for lethal crimes had his respect for all time."

A chuckle escaped as Jet absorbed this latest twist. "So, he's fond of Garrett now. Which makes me what? Grilled cheese to Garrett's steak? Robin to Garrett's Batman?"

Rain laughed, the sound touching him deep inside as well as ratcheting up his arousal.

She patted his arm. "I can't wait to tell Garrett. Oh, the look on his face when he learns he's Batman and you're the tights-wearing Boy Wonder..." She tittered all the more.

Jet rolled his eyes and swatted her rear lightly. "You're going to be a handful, I can already tell."

Rain blinked innocently up at him. "Would you want me any other way?"

He took in the sensual hunger in her eyes and blew out a breath. "No way." Unable to stop himself, he cupped her cheek, and drew her in for a kiss. The meshing of mouths started out softly and gently, a summer mist, but soon revved up with fierce passion. He opened wide, licked the seam of her lips, then plundered inside, not stopping until he'd tasted her thoroughly and she gasped for air.

After pulling back, he stared down at her, watching the myriad of expressions cross her face. "Tell me you want me."

"I want you."

The quiet words made his gut clench with need.

"But what about Garrett? I don't want to upset him again, thinking that we're going behind his back. Especially now." She worried her bottom lip and peeked up at him.

"After you left Garrett, I stayed behind for a few minutes. He ordered me to take care of you, see to your needs, until he returned tomorrow." Jet grinned ruefully.

She blinked. "He gave you permission?"

He shook his head at the irony. "He *commanded* me to care for you. Seems his alpha tendencies have come out full force, especially while he's confined to bed."

A slow grin appeared on her face. "I think you chose well in mates."

Jet's shoulders relaxed with her words. "I picked the best."

"Garrett is a keeper."

He bent down and brushed his lips over hers. "I was talking about you too."

"Oh." Her eyes brightened with desire.

"Then let's get inside where it's more comfortable."

She hesitated.

He paused and stared down at her, trying to figure out what notions ran through her head by the expression on her face. Uncertainty ranked up there.

"I will never push you into something you don't want to do."

She nodded. "I know. It's just that…"

"What?" Concern rose to a lump in his throat. He sensed her ambivalence and wanted more than anything to wipe every worry away.

Rain lifted her gaze to meet his. "I want to go for a run."

He smiled slowly. "Then that's what we'll do." He opened the door to the cabin, ushered her inside then started removing clothes.

She followed suit, keeping her back to him the entire time. Shyness. He vowed to work on that small hang up of hers, build up her confidence, and let her see herself through his eyes—all in good time.

A couple of minutes later, she leaped off the front porch and dashed straight for the nearby woods, quick and agile as she navigated the terrain. Jet tagged along, keeping pace easily enough with his larger strides and bigger frame. He let his inner beast free, relished the ability to become the animal and experience playfulness while seeing the world from a different perspective.

Rain glanced back, met his gaze then barked.

He caught the challenge to a race and picked up the speed, making sure to not allow her to get out of his sight. While he didn't fret much about her safety on their home turf, he couldn't quell the instincts which demanded he watch over his mate at all times.

They hurtled through brush, sprinted up an incline, and dodged trees, Jet still hot on her heels. Finally, she skidded to a halt, stood panting, and eyed him with sultry interest. Bowing, she assumed the wolf position for play.

He pounced, and she danced away, nipping lightly at his thick coat of fur. He faked left, then lunged right, colliding with Rain as she tried to leap aside. Instinctively, he mouthed her neck to settle her down then licked at her muzzle.

She responded in kind, watching him with those lavender eyes full of need.

His body responded instantly.

In a flash, he switched back to human form, smiling when she did so as well.

Her nude body stole his breath, jacked up his desire, and made him forget anything and everything but sinking balls deep in her body and fucking her until she screamed his name in ecstasy. Her breasts, her curves, her sparkling eyes and come hither smile. The soft supple skin which paled against the natural color of the woods.

He considered the forest floor. No way would he lay her down for the rocks, sticks and brambles to scratch her up. Same scenario with leaning her back against a tree.

Under his care, she wouldn't carry a single blemish as a result of his lovemaking, which left him with one decent option.

"Come here, baby."

Rain approached slowly then reached out to trail her fingers down his chest and straight to his aching cock. He sucked in a breath and set down a will of iron. "Care for a ride?"

Her eyebrows furrowed as she tilted her head. "How?"

He grinned, remembering her nearly untried state. "I'll show you. First things first." He sealed his mouth over hers, aggressively shoving his tongue inside and getting another taste. At the same time, he ran his hands over her body, spending extra time on her modest, yet perfect, breasts before dipping lower.

She widened her stance in order to allow him to probe between her legs. He rewarded her by slipping a digit into her moist channel.

"Hot. Tight. Wet." He added another finger. "You want me."

"Yes." She braced her hands on his shoulders and bit her lip on a gasp.

He savored the sight for a moment before reluctantly removing his touch. "I'm going to lift you up. You'll need to hold on."

Her eyes twinkled with excitement at his declaration. "Okay."

Jet bracketed her hips and lifted, juggling for a second in order to move one hand under her curvy bottom for support. With the other arm wrapped around her waist, he leaned back marginally to accommodate the position. "Guide me in, baby."

She found his cock, rubbed the tip with tender touches then nudged the head against her labia.

The second he felt her moist heat, he pressed forward while lowering her at the same time.

For only a split second, her body resisted, then he popped through, tunneling to the very depths. She cried out, a harsh sound mirroring his own.

Rain wrapped her legs around his hips and began to bounce in counter to his thrusts.

Jet knew he should go gently, but he couldn't slow down the runaway locomotive that was his arousal. He couldn't get deep enough or plunge in fast enough. He barely managed to temper his powerful strokes to avoid pounding into her. The rest, he simply let free.

His inner beast howled and yipped in excitement as he stroked in and out of Rain.

She threw her head back, her nails dug into his shoulders, as she began to whimper. The sound went straight to his balls.

"That's it, Rain. Take it. Take your pleasure from me." He growled as she nipped at his neck and gyrated with frantic intensity. He felt her muscles begin to lock under his hands as her breasts rubbed against his chest and she hung on for dear life.

Knowing she quickly approached the zenith, he let his wolf loose, really rocked his hips, and shoved deep with each motion. His back tingled from the small wounds from her nails and his knot began to tingle.

"Come on, Rain. Show me how much you like to be fucked by me."

Her breath came in hitched gasps right before she grimaced. He felt the first contraction deep within her body. The rhythmic ripples sent him right over the edge.

Slamming in once more, he felt his knot hit full size just before he shot the first stream. A hoarse shout escaped his throat as he held Rain close, locked to him in shared rapture.

By the time he finally caught his breath, Rain stared down at him with a goofy grin on her face.

"What?" He arched an eyebrow at her.

"You didn't drop me."

He snorted. "I don't know what you think about men in general, but know that I would never drop you, even when I'm coming so hard the earth shakes."

"Hmmm. Was that the earth shaking? I thought it was your knees about to give out from the extra burden of me." She peered down at him from under her lashes.

He laughed and smacked her on the rear before kissing her soundly. "Time for a dismount." Jet lifted up and pulled her free from his slowly deflating cock then returned her to her feet.

She sighed.

Concerned, he studied her for a moment. "Okay?"

"Yeah."

"Then what was that sad little sigh about?"

She blinked at him. "Oh, just thinking that when you turn to your wolf form, I'll lose the sexy eye candy."

He grinned, happy to know she found him appealing. "Want to race back and see if Garrett is having a wet dream?"

Her eyes lit up with interest. Before he could say another word, she changed to her furry form and sped off.

Jet followed suit, right on her heels all the way back to the cabin.

# Chapter Fourteen

"Home sweet home." Jet assisted Garrett through the door, carefully navigating his way around corners and obstacles to prevent his mate from even brushing his injured leg against an object.

"Finally." Garrett breathed hard from the short excursion up the front porch steps and into the living room.

Jet glanced over to find Garrett's lips thinned and his face pinched in pain. Anger rushed to the fore — again.

Today, the healer declared Garrett healthy and fit, though he'd need a few more days rest to replace the blood he'd lost and to regain his strength and stamina. In the meantime, Garrett's leg caused him quite a bit of discomfort now and again, worsening with standing for long periods bearing his own weight.

"The healer sent along some pain pills." Jet encouraged Garrett to lean on him once more as he half-lifted, half-carried him to the couch.

Garrett eased down, keeping his injured extremity stretched out straight. "No thanks. I'm fine."

Rain hurried over after shutting the door behind him. "You look a bit pale." Her face clouded in worry. "Maybe it's too soon for you to be home."

Garrett frowned up at her. "Try to drag me back to the witch doctor, and I'll throw you over my knee and spank that pretty rear until you can't sit for a week."

Rain's eyebrows shot up.

Jet smirked. "He's full of vim and vinegar today."

"Yeah, and I stink," he turned his head and sniffed near his armpit, "worse than a skunk." Using the armrest of the couch, he pushed back into a standing position.

"Now where are you going?" Rain asked.

"To the shower." He grunted and took a step, limping before Jet returned to his side, pulled Garrett's arm around his shoulder and wrapped an arm around Garrett's waist.

Jet shook his head. "Damn stubborn. Especially when he can barely walk."

Garrett paused for a second, flashing Rain a wry grin. "He can't keep his hands off me."

She chuckled.

Jet just rolled his eyes. "Let me guess. You need help in the shower."

Garrett winked at Rain. "How'd you know?"

The corner of Jet's mouth hitched up. "I'm smart like that." He tightened his hold and stepped forward. "Come on, horn dog. Let's get you clean."

Together they navigated the path to their bedroom, then into the master bathroom.

Rain watched them go, then spun around, heading directly for the kitchen. Preparing something substantial to eat was the least she could do while the guys cleaned up. Garrett looked like he could use a couple of good meals in order to regain all his strength. Jet, well, he appeared as handsome and strong as ever.

She sighed at the memory of their two times together as her belly flip-flopped. Jet knew his way around a woman's body and generously gave, ensuring she enjoyed the experience immensely. She would have sought him out more except their convoluted lives kept getting in the way.

Rain dug through the freezer, finally finding a large rump roast which sounded more her cooking speed, along with a couple of paper wrapped items marked beef stew. She picked up both, shut the lid, and returned to the kitchen. Since the roast would need to thaw, she placed it in the sink then turned her attention to the stew meat. After filling a pot with water, she turned on the stove, dumped the frozen meat in, and added some spices to the mixture. With practiced ease, she cut up potatoes, found some corn and peas, and waited for time to add the ingredients together.

"Let's get you back to bed," Jet's voice carried from the master bedroom.

Curious, she hurried down the hall, arriving at their bedroom just in time to see Garrett sink gratefully into the mattress with a deep grunt. His damp hair stuck to his head, and a few drops of water remained on his tanned skin. Garrett stretched out on his back, sighed, then relaxed into the pillows. He lay totally nude and Rain didn't mind in the least.

She stepped into the room with a smile, gently sitting on the edge of the bed beside him. Unable to keep from touching Garrett, Rain ran her hand through his hair, moving the errant locks to the side in order to be able to see his eyes.

"How are you feeling?"

He cracked one eyelid open and glanced at her. "Exhausted and damn sore."

"Not too tired for playtime in the shower, though." Jet grinned widely.

Rain blinked. "You and he—"

"Made a promise of wild, hot sex for later," Jet finished for her. "Once he was clean and had a chance to rest."

"As soon as I wake up, you mean." Garrett turned his gaze to Jet, love and excitement sparked in his eyes.

"Deal." Jet trailed his fingers over Garrett's chest, lightly caressing as if he couldn't keep his hands to himself. Silence reigned for a long moment. "You scared a century off my life, I'll have you know."

Jet stared at Garrett with such an intense expression of love and adoration, Rain felt a pinch of jealousy. Maybe one day, both men would gaze at her in such a way. If she was lucky. Damn lucky.

"That's the bravest thing I've ever heard of, Garrett. Realizing your alpha was behind it all and having the guts to do something about it." She smiled down at him, sincere in her praise. A lower status individual challenging an existing alpha was almost unheard of. To win the battle made for future legends.

"You should have waited." Jet's tone flattened. "You could've been killed because of your stubbornness."

Garrett shook his head. "My pack, my problem."

"*My* mate, *my* problem," Jet fired back.

"Both my mates make it my problem, too," Rain ventured into the conversation.

The men stared at her in astonishment for a long moment before their faces softened.

"Going to still give us a try?" Garrett reached up and took her hand in his.

She nodded. Since the injury, Garrett had been so different with her. She adored his new attitude, the attempts at charming flirting, the caring he projected onto her. He appealed to her before, but now did so ten times as much without the snarling and accusations. She found herself falling for his teasing grins, his sweetness, and his exquisite body.

"How could I not? I have these two sexy men who are willing to put their lives on the line to help me and protect their own. That makes me one very lucky woman."

The corner of Jet's mouth hitched up.

Garrett eyed her with amusement. "Good thing this bed is big enough for all of us." He patted the mattress beside him. "Climb on board."

Rain arched an eyebrow and shared a look with Jet. "Uh-uh. I believe you have a promise to uphold to Jet right after your nap."

"Party pooper." Garrett pouted until a wide yawn ruined the effect.

She leaned in and kissed his cheek. "That's right. I have food to cook. You need your rest to keep up with Jet." She glanced up to find Jet staring at her with a mixture of relief, happiness, and longing.

"But I want you both." Garrett squeezed her hand.

She stared at him for a moment, made a decision, and answered truthfully. "And you'll have me. Later. Once you're healed and back on your feet."

Pulling her hand from Garrett's, she smiled at Jet then slid off the bed. A few steps later, she left the room, leaving Jet to watch over their mate as he slept.

Jet emerged from the bedroom several minutes later and headed directly for the kitchen, entering as Rain stirred the stew.

"He's sleeping."

"Good. Poor guy needs it." Rain rinsed her knife off in the sink.

"The healer said another day or three and he'd be back to new." He opened the door to the pantry, pulled out a box, and opened the top.

Rain glanced at the item, then grinned. "Baking a cake?"

Jet grinned sheepishly. "Garrett has a sweet tooth. He loves yellow cake."

"Minus the chocolate icing?"

"You got it." Jet pulled a bowl from the cabinet and began mixing the ingredients together.

Rain watched him work, noting the strong hands, the sureness of each move. His toned body made her mouth water even as his quick wit challenged her. Jet made her feel comfortable, yet aroused at the same time. A definite enigma.

"You didn't know Garrett's an alpha when you met?"

Jet shook his head as he added water to the dry cake powder. "He kept that secret—very well too. Thinking back now, there were plenty of signs, if only I paid attention. The fact is, I was too attracted to him, too fired up, and we couldn't pry ourselves away from one another. We got along just fine, so nothing else mattered."

"And now? Will his being an alpha change anything?" She whispered the question as she cleaned up the peelings and placed them in a bucket to take out to the compost pile later.

"Not really. Garrett's who he's always been. The fact that he jumped up a status doesn't change the way I feel, nor does it affect our relationship. He's been an alpha since we met, and it's worked out well. I don't think anything will be different. I'm still going to push him around now and again. That's me. He tolerates it. That's just his personality."

She absorbed this information. "So you're on equal footing now?"

He pinned her with his gaze. "We've always been on equal footing, Rain. I respect Garrett. There's no need for titles and rules based on status in this house. As far as I'm concerned, we're all on the same level. Period." Jet punched buttons on the bottom oven then grabbed a large wooden spoon out of a nearby drawer.

"But in Horizon..."

Jet set down his stirring spoon then reached out to gently cup Rain's chin. He meshed his lips with hers. "Sweetheart, you're no longer there. Spring Hill is different. *We're* different. If you haven't realized that by now, we've got a lifetime to convince you."

She blinked at Jet, savored the small amount of affection that left her wanting more. She opened her mouth then closed it once more. He spelled things out so simply that sometimes her mind sped by, then had to slam on the brakes.

"We're all the same?"

He grinned wickedly. "In status, yes. In other things, no."

She tilted her head in question.

"One of us has delightful curves, beautiful breasts, and a perfect pussy just made for loving."

Rain's face heated. Her body responded immediately with a clenching of her stomach and a tingle of need between her legs.

The bottom oven dinged.

"We'll find time to pleasure you again. Soon." Jet kissed her quickly then went back to stirring with a vengeance.

# Chapter Fifteen

"Are you supposed to be washing windows?" Rain's voice would have startled him if he hadn't detected her light flowery scent first.

"It's fine. Hell, the healer said I'm fit as a fiddle and could even return to security duty. Jet's the one being a stubborn mule and forbidding me from returning to work for a few more days."

He finished wiping the master bedroom window and turned to Rain. "That's why he asked you to hang around the house for a few days—to babysit me and make sure I didn't do anything too strenuous." He rolled his eyes.

Rain giggled. "Considering you scared us both to death, I don't blame Jet in the least."

He smiled at her amusement. The past couple of days had been an adventure and learning experience for him concerning his newest mate. Rain continually surprised him with her generosity, her sense of humor, even her subtle flirting. He'd been blind to the goodness inside her before but cherished her unique traits now. She worked just as hard as they did to keep the house clean, to cook three meals per day, and to make the new relationship work. She'd even postponed her return to her home and business until he'd regained all his strength to everyone's satisfaction. If he had his way, she'd find a way to stay with them and run her business from a distance.

He arched an eyebrow at her. "You gonna tie me down like Jet threatened to?"

She blushed and shook her head. "No one ever mentioned you guys were kinky."

"Oh, you have no idea." He waggled his eyebrows at her.

She chuckled. "Flirting will get you nowhere."

He sniffed dramatically. "You sure about that?" Garrett only meant to lightly tease, not wanting to put the least amount of sexual pressure on her. As far as he knew, Jet had only taken her a couple of times, and Garrett hadn't yet. In his eyes, that made her just about as innocent as one could get. Considering the rollercoaster they'd all been on the past couple of weeks, he counted his blessings that she'd stuck around, let alone chipped in while he recovered.

When she hesitated, he placed a peck on her cheek. "You're so fun to tease." He found the words to be the truth. She gave back much of the time. Others, she seemed to sputter through her embarrassment—a continuous source of amusement for him and Jet.

With a quick wink, he returned to his task.

"Garrett?"

He turned from inspecting the window for streaks to look at her.

She sucked in a breath and pushed her shoulders back, as if trying to gain confidence in order to say what was on her mind. "I want to take you and Jet both at the same time. But I've never..." Her words trailed off. She glanced down, then back up to meet his gaze steadily. "I've never had anal sex before. I thought...maybe you...will you teach me?"

The enormity of her request humbled him. She had been an innocent when Jet had first covered her. Now, she was asking him to take her other virginity, to penetrate her in a way no one ever had before. His heart pounded even as his cock leaped to attention in response. The thought of shoving balls deep in her curvy rear made him salivate and his already revved-up libido skyrocket with longing.

"Are you sure?"

She bit her lip but nodded. "Yes. I want you this way. Please?"

He puffed out a breath, set aside the paper towels and glass cleaner, before taking both her hands in his. "Then I'll be honored to initiate you, little one."

She smiled, then lifted to tiptoe in order to brush a kiss across his lips. "Thank you."

He chuckled and wrapped her in his embrace, sealing their lips together in a precursor of the events to come. She opened her mouth as he flicked his tongue over hers, greedily asking for every ounce of passion she possessed. When she tangled her tongue with his, he groaned in response, already fired up and hungry for more.

After grabbing the hem of her shirt, he tugged, breaking apart in order to remove the garment. He immediately cupped a bra-clad breast, learning the shape and size. He kissed her again, aggressively meeting her tongue and tapping for a quick game of tag. Only the need for air broke them apart the second time.

"Damn." Garrett reached around to unsnap her bra, watching as Rain slipped the straps off herself. A perfect nipple topped each beautiful, perky breast. His mouth watered for a taste.

Before he had a chance to swoop down and pay homage to her bosom, Rain reached for his shirt, yanked it over his head then made quick work of the buttons of his jeans. He finished pulling them down then kicked the unwanted denim aside. By the time he stood still once more, Rain's hands found his erection, wrapped lovingly around, and measured him tip to base.

Garrett groaned as arrows of pleasure shot through him at her delicate touch. He curled his lips back as he set his back teeth, determined to hold fast to his control until she reached climax at least once. No rushing first times.

He circled her wrist in a loose bracelet and pulled her hands away in order to go to work on her pants. Efficiently, he unsnapped the top button then unzipped the zipper. As soon as the material loosened, he delved his hand inside, cupping the junction between her legs.

"You're already wet." He wiggled his fingers over the soft cotton panties. "Very wet."

Rain gasped and looked up at him with hooded eyes. "I want you. Badly."

Her words spurred his arousal that much more. He lectured himself to go slow, to make this initial experience a delightful and decadent memory for Rain.

She hooked her thumbs in her pants and underwear, then shimmied them down to puddle at her ankles. Gracefully, she stepped out of the discarded clothing to stand totally nude before him.

His breath caught. While petite, Rain had curves in all the right places. Modest breasts stood proud.

Flaring hips and a flat belly followed. A sprinkling of dark brown curls protected her femininity. Athletic legs completed the beautiful package—perfection in his opinion.

Her gaze met his. Her eyes spoke of hunger, need, and a flash of awe as she appraised his body before focusing on his face once more. "No wonder Jet picked you." She reached out to trace her fingers over his nipple, lightly rubbing until the button drew taut. "You're gorgeous."

"Not half as much as you." He embraced her, drawing their bodies flush as he peppered kisses along her jaw, her temple, then down to her earlobe, which he lightly nipped.

Rain pressed her chest into his body and wrapped her arms around his neck, her short nails already digging into the skin of his back. The mild discomfort told of her arousal and added more fuel to the fiery blaze in his blood.

"On the bed."

She backed away, tugging him with her. Then she twisted, climbed on the mattress, and crawled until she reached the middle.

He growled at the sight of her rounded rear wiggling with each step. His wolf whimpered, clamoring for him to mount her already, make her his. Garrett grappled with his instincts for a long moment, not moving until he had his urges firmly in hand. After stepping to the bedside table, he dug out a bottle of lube, and tossed it on the bed.

As much as he wanted to slide balls deep in her ass, he chided himself to slow down and ensure her absolute readiness. *Foreplay.*

"Flip over." He watched as she turned to him with an expression of puzzlement. She didn't ask, only did as he commanded.

He smiled as he moved toward her, stopping at her feet. "Now, open your legs."

She did so. Marginally.

"More, baby. Let me see that pretty pussy of yours."

Rain blushed, which only added to her radiance. She splayed farther, far enough for him to easily settle in between. "That's it." He leaned over and kissed her stomach, even as he slipped one finger inside her snug folds. "You're soaking my finger, baby."

She arched, pressing closer, as if needing more than a single digit. He gave her more in the form of a second finger, easily sliding in beside the first. The heady scent of her arousal ratcheted him all the higher. He lowered to his stomach, adjusted his position then ran his tongue between her swollen labia.

Rain mewled and more juice covered his fingers still buried deep inside. He repeated the action, this time dipping his tongue into her slit before trailing upward, locating her clit then deliberately licking across.

She cried out, bucked, and began to pant. "More. Oh please more."

He laved the area while moving his fingers in a preview of what was to come. As soon as her body tightened, he backed off, completely removing his touch. He wanted her stretched on a rack of passion when he finally sunk into her. He could eat her out all day long, the taste so divine, but moved in cautious steps. If she hit orgasm now, she might not be as needy or desperate when he penetrated her.

A grunt of disappointment followed. He grinned to himself. Let her teeter on the edge of fulfillment for the moment. Her state would only help them both when he finally moved to cover her.

"Garrett?"

He sat up and glanced down at her. "Yes, Rain?"

"I need more."

After stretching over her, he kissed the pout off her lips. "I know, baby. You'll get more. But we need to do a bit more preparation first." He drew back enough to see her face clearly. "Unless you've changed your mind?"

She shook her head, her brunette locks spreading over the pillow. "No. I want you to take me. Back there."

He scooted back. "Then turn over for me." He plucked the tube off the bed, opened the cap, and squirted a generous amount on his fingers. He watched Rain as she rolled over then went up on hands and knees, facing away from him. His cock jumped and began to throb at the vision she created.

Slowly he trailed one hand down her back and caressed her rear, learning the texture of her silky skin. "Beautiful."

Edging closer, he began to spread the cool gel in the crack, focusing his attention on the small opening. "Spread your legs more and put your head down."

She lowered her upper body and adjusted. The new position provided an easy target and perfect vantage point of the spot he intended to penetrate soon. "Just like that."

After lining up one digit with her hole, he pressed steadily inside. Her sphincter resisted for a moment before opening just enough to allow him entrance. He sank as deeply as possible and began to massage the muscle, to coat the walls, spreading the needed lubrication all around. In. Out. Circle around. Garrett worked the area thoroughly, providing encouragement along the way. After pulling back, he added a second finger and pushed them in together.

Rain sucked in air but held steady. Carefully, he spread his fingers, easing the tension.

"Are we ready?" She panted out the question.

"I need to stretch you some more, baby." He used his free hand to dip below, found her channel, and sank his fingers deep.

She jerked back, trying to hump herself on his fingers.

He smiled at her reaction. Dripping wet, she enjoyed this play as much as he did. His ego bolstered as his cock became more insistent with painful need.

"Garrett." His name came out as a long moan.

He removed his fingers from both her channels, found the lube, and poured a generous dollop on his hand, then stroked himself a couple of times to spread the gel. One more squeeze of the tube and he tossed it aside. Then, he clamped three fingers together and he pushed back into her hole.

She sighed as her body opened more, welcoming him back with the assistance of the lube.

Unable to wait a moment more, Garrett moved closer, took his cock in hand, and lined himself up with her waiting entrance. "Just relax." With those words, he began to press forward with exquisite control. Her muscular ring resisted the larger penetration. Patiently, he applied the same gentle pressure, waiting for her body to relent. "Push back, Rain."

She did and grunted as he popped through.

Pausing, he stroked her back, giving her a chance to acclimate to his presence in a place no other man had been. He reached around, molded a breast with a lazy caress before tunneling his fingers between her folds again. Immediately, he found her clit and strummed over the area.

She writhed under his touch, impaling herself farther in her attempts to force more attention on the sensitive bundle of nerves. "That's it. Just keep pushing back."

He flicked over the taut area again. While he pushed at the same time, she lurched back, and he gained another couple of inches.

Rain sucked in air.

Garrett stalled, finding the tightest core he'd ever ventured into. Heat wrapped around him as the snug walls gripped him like a velvet fist, setting off cherry bombs in his nearly out of control fire. He ran multiplication tables in his mind—anything to distract him from coming way too soon.

"How much more?" Rain asked on an uptake of air.

"Not much." He worked her clit again, surged ahead then abandoned the sensual torment in order to clamp down on her hips. "Almost there." By tiny increments, he pulled her toward him, lodging himself deeper and deeper. Sweat broke out on his back as he struggled to hold the snail's pace.

She whimpered and grunted, arching abruptly a time or two when he proceeded too quickly.

He knew exactly how she felt, welcoming the cock that could give so much pleasure, yet struggling with the pain of penetration. He'd been there many times before. Sultry need always won out with a gentle and patient lover.

With two more tiny thrusts, he bottomed out, seated fully in her depths. Garrett stroked her back, then down her sides. "That's it. You've got it all."

She shivered beneath his touch and whimpered. She clamped down tighter than he thought possible before easing just slightly.

For the longest time, he remained still, giving her plenty of time to adjust, waiting for a definite signal she was ready for more. In the meantime, he brushed his hands over her exposed body, dipped between her legs, and did his damnedest to assist her acceptance of his large dick comfortably. He lost track of time as he showered her with attention.

"Okay?"

She released a pent-up breath and pushed back almost hesitantly. "I think so." Her words lacked conviction.

"Let's try this. Tell me if I hurt you." With tender care, he retreated a couple of inches before reversing course at the speed of a fat caterpillar. When Rain moaned, he repeated the action. "Still all right?"

"Yes. Oh, yes." Her hands fisted in the sheets as she threw her head back. Her pelvis tilted with his next thrust, absorbing his stroke as deeply as possible.

Grasping onto her hips with both hands, Garrett set a slow pace, moving in short strokes, maximizing her pleasure while always aware of her untried state. "Hurt?"

She shook her head. "Not any more. It's just…"

"Too much?"

"No. Not near enough. I need more. Something more." She countered his next push forward by shoving, causing their bodies to slap together. "More of that."

"You're going to make me come, baby. Tell me now. Knot in or out."

"In." She didn't even hesitate to answer.

"That's the way I want it too. Tied up in your ass." Garrett took her words to heart and began to pick up speed even as he lengthened his strokes. Pulling almost all the way out, he shoved back in, not stopping until he couldn't go any farther. In. Out. In. Out. A tingling began at the base of his spine. He ground his back teeth, stemming the inevitable for as long as possible. Rain had to reach the pinnacle first.

His whole world centered on the woman under him. He leaned forward, covered her body with his own, his hips continuing to move as he licked across the nape of her neck. The gland began to swell in his cock, sending another wave of bliss over him.

"Come for me, baby. I need for you to come."

She whimpered, splayed her legs farther apart, and slammed back against him. Her head fell to the bed as she drew in great gasps of air, moaned, and finally cried out.

Garrett kept up the pressure, pushing her to the very edge, needing for her to fall over so he could follow. "That's it. Stick that ass up in the air. Take my cock." He sought her cleft once more, found her taut clit, and very lightly pinched.

She tightened like a bowstring. Again he plucked at her nub.

With an inarticulate cry, she shoved backward as the first contractions squeezed his cock tighter than a vise. The additional stimulation, along with the knowledge that his mate reached orgasm under him, sent him right over the edge. He shoved in as deeply as possible just as his knot swelled fully, locking them together as one. The first volley of semen soon followed. He knew it was the first of many spurts to come during their time tied together.

Instinctively, he nuzzled her shoulder, then sank his fangs deep, both holding her in place as well as cranking up his pleasure another notch. His inner wolf howled with excitement at finally claiming his mate the way a female wolf shifter should be taken, his body over hers.

He growled as more seed released from his body into hers. Each one brought another explosion of bliss through him and his throbbing dick. Her ass clenched and gripped him tight as the rhythmic spasms of her climax continued.

Garrett rode the tides of rapture with glee.

Feeling prying eyes watching, Garrett angled his head, not releasing his hold on Rain's nape. He found Jet leaning against the doorjamb, his gaze locked on Garrett and Rain. Totally naked, Jet stroked his erect cock. Even as he watched, a drop of moisture appeared at the tip. The sight only whetted his desire and sent another wave of bright, burning pleasure through him.

"Damn, that was hot."

# Chapter Sixteen

Rain tensed at the voice and glanced to her right, instinctively jerking against Garrett's knot with surprise. Her gasp turned into a whimper as she quaked with the ongoing climax.

Garrett stroked her soothingly as her inner muscles squeezed his still spurting member so tightly the sensation bordered on discomfort. Gently, he retracted his fangs from her skin and licked his lips as he panted for breath, his eyes never leaving Jet's gorgeous body.

Garrett grinned wickedly. "You should see and feel it from my perspective."

"I believe I will." After walking over, he ran his hands through Rain's silky locks, cupped Garrett's head and tugged him close for a kiss full of passion and need. Mouth open, Jet took the aggressive approach, flicking over Garrett's teeth, asking for a taste.

Garrett moaned at the affection, which only heightened his ecstasy as his cock jumped and released another stream of semen deep inside Rain's channel.

"Still knotted?" Jet whispered against Garrett's lips.

"Yeah."

"Good. That'll give Rain time to suck on my aching cock before she climbs aboard."

Jet gave Garrett one more peck on the lips before scooting around until the headboard supported his upper body, along with a couple of added pillows for comfort.

Splaying his legs, he gestured to Rain. "Come on, baby. I've been aching for your tongue on my dick for a long time."

All Rain had to do was lean forward, which she did immediately.

Garrett watched from his kneeling position as Jet wrapped his fingers around the base of his impressive erection and pointed the tip toward Rain. Her dainty tongue flicked over the end, sending a wave of pleasure across Jet's face. She opened wide and took the mushroomed head in her mouth.

Jet groaned in harmony with Garrett, as another wave of rapture cascaded through him, aided by the stimulating scene right before his eyes. He'd never seen a more exciting sight than Jet being pleasured orally by Rain, her mouth encompassing as much of the shaft as possible, obviously sending shocks of delight through him by the way he moaned, grabbed her hair, and pulled her closer.

"So damn good." Jet threw his head back.

With one more glorious clench and spurt, Garrett's knot subsided, allowing him to carefully withdraw from Rain.

After moving forward, he nuzzled her ear, sucking on the lobe for a second before whispering. "Are you okay?"

She paused for a moment in her ministrations, letting Jet's cock fall out of her mouth to glance in his direction with a wide grin. "More than okay. Wonderful." Her eyes danced.

With a relieved sigh, he leaned in close and lapped at Jet's dick along with Rain. Together they showered him with affection before he finally nudged them away. "Enough. Any more of that and I'll come."

"So?" Garrett smiled and tilted his head to lick the bead of dew off Jet's leaking tip.

Jet sucked in a breath. "I'd much rather come inside Rain than on the damn sheets." He growled and adjusted positions until he lay spread out on the bed, his upper body supported by thick pillows. The angle allowed him to watch the action while providing ample room for Rain to avoid banging her head on the wooden board at the front end of the bed.

Garrett sat back on his heels, watched and waited. He licked his lips as Rain gracefully straddled Jet, allowing him to guide her into proper alignment. The motion granted him a clear view of full pink inner lips glistening with moisture along with her back opening, which he already needed to explore again. His cock jumped at the visual, quickly filling back up to full mast, despite his recent orgasm.

"Come on, baby. Climb on board."

"What about Garrett?" Rain twisted her neck to look at him. "I need Garrett too."

His heart buoyed, even as his once more full erection throbbed. With a reassuring smile, Garrett reached out to trail his fingers down her straight spine. "It's okay. I'm right here and not going anywhere soon." Moving closer, he sealed his lips over hers, slipped his tongue inside as she gasped, and thoroughly tasted. "Do you want me at the same time as Jet?"

She worried her bottom lip for a second. "Yes. If there's any way possible, I want you both at the same time."

"Oh, it's possible." Jet extended his hand and cupped the junction between Rain's thighs. "Entirely possible. If we go slow and easy."

Garrett seconded Jet's advice. "I don't want to hurt you and you might be sore already."

"I'm fine. More than fine." She sucked in air as Jet's fingers slid deep between her folds. "I. Need. You. Both. Now."

Jet chuckled and removed his digits. "Then settle down on me, sweetheart. I can't wait to feel your heat again."

Garrett couldn't tear his gaze away as she ever so slowly pushed downward, accepting Jet's huge erection into her petite body. She paused halfway, took a couple of slow deep breaths, and continued on her journey until she sat on Jet's hips, his cock fully embedded in her pussy.

"Damn, you're tight." Jet grasped her hips and held her steady before releasing her long enough to cup the back of her head and pull her down for a sizzling kiss. "Just hold still until Garrett's settled," he whispered against her lips then cradled a full breast in the palm of his hand.

Tightening the reins of his control, Garrett grabbed the earlier discarded lube, squirted a generous dollop on his hand then rubbed his fingers in the slippery goo. Only when they were fully coated did he tenderly insert first one finger into her anus, then added another. In and out he pushed before twirling his wrist to get her sphincter to relax again.

Rain moaned and pushed back, her body asking for more.

Garrett repeated the action for a couple of minutes before removing his fingers and using the leftover lubricant to slicken his once again granite hard erection. "Relax, Rain. Just hold still and let me do the work."

Jet grabbed her rear and spread her cheeks wide, giving Garrett an easy target to aim for. "That's it, baby. Suck my nipple."

After lining his tip with her upturned rear, Garrett softly pushed, holding steady pressure until her anus relented, opening wide to allow his entrance. The muscular ring provided a brief resistance then he popped through.

Rain grunted and gasped, tensing for a split second.

"Easy, sweetheart. We're in no hurry." Garrett tried to coax her, ease her pain and concerns while holding rigid control over his arousal. He'd give her all the time in the world she needed in order to accept them both without discomfort. When the tightness eased a smidgen, he pressed forward once more, millimeters at a time, gaining another three inches before stopping.

Jet clasped her hips so hard the skin blanched. "Shit. I can feel your cock rubbing against mine." His breathing accelerated. "That's so hot. So fucking good."

Garrett bent forward and kissed Rain's nape, licking over the small wound where his fangs had sunk deep not long ago. "Almost there, baby." He bunched his muscles and began again, not planning on stopping until he hit bottom. She was just as tight as the first time around, though this time they both knew she could not only accept his long and thick cock, she could reach the pinnacle with his skillful technique as he pumped in and out of her.

She grunted, shivered, and arched her back. A small whimper escaped from her throat.

Jet pulled her face up for a deep kiss, effectively distracting her for the rest of Garrett's penetration.

"You've got it all." He immediately reached around, found where she and Jet were joined, then tunneled his fingers until he brushed across her clit. She jerked at his touch, even as the harsh tightness of her back channel loosened a hair.

"All right?" Jet asked.

She panted for a moment. "Yes. Oh, yes. So full. So much of you both. I need more. Something more." She rocked her hips.

Both men moaned at the sensation.

Jet met Garrett's gaze over Rain's head as she nibbled her way up his neck and to his ear. "Notice the scent?"

For a moment, Garrett stared at his mate in confusion. Then his olfactory senses picked up what Jet detected—a highly erotic smell, one that stoked his lust to a full-blown blaze and threatened to snap his normally exquisite control.

"She's in heat." He made the words a statement.

"I'm what?" She froze, both palms planted on Jet's wide chest.

"In heat," Jet answered with a grin. "It seems our play has sent you right into heat."

"Oh, hell." She shoved back and rotated her pelvis, stroking Garrett's cock in all the right places while allowing him to feel Jet's endowment right below, the organ lodged deep in her depths. "What does that mean, exactly?" Her words took on a breathless tone.

Garrett chuckled and ran his hands up and down her back with growing familiarity. "It means we're mated, baby. And we're going to have one hell of a ride for the next day or two."

She groaned dramatically then gasped as Garrett pulled back a couple of inches only to punch back in. He repeated the motion then established a see-saw rhythm with Jet, one moving forward, the other back, as they gently initiated Rain into their mated sandwich. Moans filled the air as together they worked toward a unified peak. Garrett set his back teeth, grasped onto his control with an iron fist, needing his mates to hit strong orgasms before he released once more.

Rain twisted enough to look up at him, her eyes hooded as she panted in need. He covered her back completely. After sealing his lips over hers, he drank in her essence followed by her high pitched cry of impending rapture. He arched his back and added more power to his thrusts, keeping the pace steady, yet plundering the depths of her ass as far as he could penetrate. Gentleness guided his motions.

Jet's rock hard erection brushed against his, back and forth, adding to the nearly overwhelming stimulation of taking their mate at the same time. Each stroke added more friction from Jet's member, even as Rain's lubrication-aided channel clenched him tightly, the tiniest movement adding another element of snugness, squeezing and liquid heat.

"Shit. I'm going to come," Jet announced with a half growl.

Rain whimpered, pulled back from Garrett's kiss, and braced herself against Jet's chest, no longer moving counter to their thrusts.

Garret realized why a moment later as he shoved in, only to feel Jet's knot bulging beneath him. "Damn." He sucked in a breath, shoved as deep as possible, then reached around to strum Rain's taut clit. Once. Twice. A third time. She tightened like a bow string as strong contractions caressed his buried cock like a velvet hand, welcoming him, demanding everything he had to give.

With an inarticulate cry, his knot swelled, locking him deep inside Rain's depths, just behind the area Jet's gland still jerked. She shuddered and quaked, gasped and cried out, her body continuing the deep massage of both their rods, kicking his already strong climax up another notch. If she experienced pain from the added burden of their tied up status, he couldn't tell. Not with her body's eager responses. The individual aroma of her heat soaked into his pores, into his very soul, and compelled him to greater heights.

Garrett found the junction of her neck and shoulder and sank his teeth deep, marking her with a wound that matched the one he'd made minutes before. Absently, he noticed Jet did the same, holding her in place with their bites as they continued to empty their loads in her.

All too soon, his knot began to deflate. Garrett unclamped his jaws and returned to a kneeling position, relieving Rain of his weight. He noticed that Jet followed suit, nuzzling Rain's cheek as he leaned back on the pillows and stared at them both, a well satisfied expression written clearly on his face.

"Talk about intense."

"Definitely the best. Ever." With infinite care, Garrett grasped Rain's hips and slowly began to ease out, feeling her flinch before he managed to extricate himself. Probably already sore, she'd be more so in the morning, unless her hormones kicked in enough to override the discomfort she most likely felt—certainly possible from what he'd heard about full-blown heat in wolf shifter females.

Rain softly mewled and sat back, balancing herself on Jet's hips. "I never knew how good that could be." She rocked on Jet's member. "Garrett?" Rain called for him with almost a desperate quality to her voice.

He scooted around beside Jet, where she could see him. Unable to resist temptation, he covered one breast with his hand and flicked his thumb over the taut nipple. "I'm right here, Rain."

She sighed and leveled her gaze at him. "Don't go anywhere. Please. Stay. I need you."

He smiled up at her. "I'm not going anywhere, baby. Not without you and Jet by my side."

Her body trembled as she smiled lovingly at him. "I think I've fallen for you." She pressed her lips to his before adjusting her position and did the same for Jet. "And for you, too." She kissed him then sat back up with a wry grin on her face. "I can't believe how lucky I am. The best mates in the world are mine." She writhed on top of Jet, causing his hips to buck.

"We're the lucky ones," Garrett answered, as Jet blew out a long breath of air.

"If you don't slow down, I'll be spent in thirty seconds," Jet warned as he reached over, cupped the back of Garrett's head, and meshed their lips together. Aggressively, he shoved his tongue in Garrett's mouth, seeking and pillaging along the way. Garrett pinched Jet's nipple, then grinned as his first mate nearly roared with another quick rise to the precipice before tumbling over.

By the time Jet caught his breath, Rain had lifted off and snuggled up against Garrett's side, resting her head in his lap.

"You two have worn me out."

"Us?" Garrett stroked her hair away from her face. "I think you've worn us out."

Jet grinned at them both. "We can argue about it later. Much later."

Garrett glanced from Rain's passion-covered face to Jet. Their eyes met as they shared a knowing look. He felt it too. The bonding, the absolute knowledge they had found their third—for now and for a lifetime to come.

# Chapter Seventeen

Rain woke to the sensation of her legs being nudged apart. Still half asleep, she didn't utter a protest, simply drifted back toward her dreams, until a raspy tongue licked straight down her slit.

Fully awake, heat and lust returned in force. If she believed the threesome a few hours before fulfilled the immense needs of her hormones, this morning proved her wrong. Totally wrong.

Her breath hitched with the next delicate exploration as she opened her eyes only to find Jet leaning over her with a wicked grin on his face.

"Good morning, Rain." He palmed a breast and absently flicked the nipple.

She opened her mouth to speak, but only a groan emerged as Garrett fastened his mouth over her tender clit and began laving with intent. Her hips jerked in response as she latched onto Jet's wrist, holding his touch on her aching breast. "Oh, yes. Yesssss." Pulling her legs up and out, she made ample room for Garrett as he cupped her bottom and lifted her pelvis to create more friction. A sharp whimper tore from her throat at the dual pleasures.

Garrett lifted his head and stared at her, his mouth slick with her juices. "Good morning, mate."

Her heart thumped against her ribs at the sex appeal of both men, but especially Garrett, planted between her legs, eagerly tasting her.

"How do you feel this morning?" Jet drew her attention back to him with a soft squeeze of her breast and a kiss to her collar bone.

"Needy. Hot and oh so needy." The slightly hoarse words punctuated with a wordless cry as Garrett's fingers slid into her hungry folds.

"That's what we wanted to hear." Jet grinned wickedly.

She began to pant. "Is this the way it's supposed to be. My previous heat wasn't anything like this." Rain raised her gaze to Jet's, searching for answers while shockwaves of escalating pleasure coursed through her body.

He stroked her hair and bent over to kiss her on the lips, tunneling his tongue inside, exploring briefly, then sitting back. His cock stood at attention, jutting straight out from his body.

She noted the bead of moisture on the tip and couldn't resist reaching out, catching the drop with her finger, then tasting.

Jet's eyes narrowed as he watched. "We're true mates, baby. That would explain why the heat, a true mating heat, would be more intense. Not to mention you have us here to not only see to every one of your needs, but to stimulate you for more."

Garrett pressed the tips of his fingers upward in her pussy, brushing over a hot spot. She cried out, grabbed his head with one hand and tried to press him closer. "It's not enough." Her voice broke as she arched, twitched, and gyrated. Nothing helped alleviate the almost boiling need overtaking her body.

"Shhh." Jet straddled her, blocking her view of Garrett with his large body. His black eyes snapped in hunger and promise. "You're killing me with those sexy little sounds, baby."

He reached out with his fingers. She opened wide and sucked them in, treating them like she would his gorgeous dick. Glancing up, she found his jaw taut and his cock twitching. She wrapped her fingers around his shaft, then ran her hand down his length, giving a snug squeeze, before returning to the tip.

Upon removing his fingers, he grabbed the base of his dick. "Suck me baby. Get me all wet and ready for Garrett."

She didn't have to be told twice. As soon as he lifted and braced his weight on the bed above her head, she grasped his cock, and pulled it to her lips. She snaked her tongue out and worried the slit, begging for more pre-cum. He groaned and arched his back, pushing more of his rod into her mouth. She greedily lashed her tongue over every inch while slipping her hand under his body. After finding his low hanging sac, she fondled his balls then gave them a tentative pull.

Jet growled and jerked. "Shit, yes."

"Mmmm." She purred and licked the vibrations rushing over Jet's erection. Her breath catching as Garrett stuffed a finger into her rear. With a sharp cry, she arched, getting much closer, but still not quite where she needed to be. Distracted, she tried to split her attention between her aching cleft, her throbbing clit, Garrett's slight invasion of her ass, and Jet's superb, tasty dick in her mouth.

Jet cradled the back of her head, lifting. "Suck, Rain. Suck my cock."

The new angle crammed more of his thick fullness into her mouth. Her cheeks hollowed as she added vacuum pressure. He cussed, he jumped and groaned. His hips thrust ever so slightly, as if he tried to hold back but couldn't stop the motion completely.

Stretched on a rack of passion, Rain noticed her world had narrowed down to the two men showering her with rich affection.

Jet moved, taking her delicious cock with him. She whimpered.

He pressed a quick kiss to her lips. "Garrett's turn, sweetheart. Don't worry. We've got plenty of time and he's not about to stop licking your pretty pussy." He slid off the bed, opened a drawer, grabbed up a tube of lube then walked to the end of the bed. She watched as he squirted some gel on his fingers then slid them into Garrett's upturned rear while Garrett continued to play deep inside her own body.

A couple of minutes of the chain reaction and she gripped the comforter with both fists, her attention focused on the erotic play between the two men, even as Garrett kept her near the brink with his tormenting tongue.

She growled in frustration as he lifted his head from the spot she needed him the most, leaving only his fingers busily exploring her two holes. "Patience, love."

Jet greased up his cock then set the tip against Garrett's opening, bracing his hands on Garrett's lower back. He paused for a long moment, his gaze locking with Rain's. He wrapped his arms around Garrett's middle and pulled him upward until Garrett sat on his heels. Then Jet plundered Garrett's mouth, before trailing kisses along Garrett's jawline and around to his earlobe.

"I think Rain needs something more than finger fucking right now."

Garrett grinned wickedly as he looked down at her.

Her stomach clenched in delight at the sensual promise written clearly on his face.

"Uh huh. I'm thinking we might need to put you in the middle of a sandwich."

Garrett groaned deep and long. His full erection bobbed.

Rain licked her lips, Jet's suggestion already lashing up her arousal tenfold.

"What do you think, Rain?" Jet asked, as he nibbled Garrett's ear some more.

"I think it's a great idea." She scooted down and adjusted the pillow for comfort. "Come on, Garrett. You've kept me waiting long enough."

Both men chuckled.

"She's going to be demanding." Garrett whispered, as he turned his head and accepted Jet's kiss.

"Already is." Jet released him with a gentle nudge. "Go on. Claim her so I can bring up the rear of the party."

Garrett complied, scooting to the open area between her thighs. He stretched out, bracing his hands on either side of her shoulders, then leaned down to mesh their lips.

Responding instantly, Rain accepted Garrett's questing tongue with exuberance. He tapped hers then reacquainted himself with every nook and cranny, leaving her breathless.

He lifted his head and peered down at her. She felt his entry, slow and sure, gradually filling her in the place she needed attention the most. Her folds welcomed him with snugness as he burrowed to the deepest penetration possible.

"Okay?"

She smiled softly up at him, touched by his concern. "More than okay."

He matched her grin and rocked against her. "Like that, do ya?"

"Yessss. Oh, yes." She wrapped her arms around his back, lifted her legs to bracket his hips, opening herself farther for Garrett's strokes.

She met his gaze, saw the flare in his eyes, and heard his grunt as Jet shoved him marginally forward with his presumed entry into Garrett's body. She cupped his face, trailing her fingers over his full lips. "Does it hurt?"

He shook his head and kissed her fingertips. "Just a bit of spice to add in with the sweetness."

She pulled him down and sealed her lips over his, needing to give him as much pleasure as he gave her, both now and last night.

"That's it, baby. Now, let me lead." Jet's voice carried to her ears just before an easy rolling motion began.

Garrett made love to her with short, gentle jabs, rubbing all her hot spots while licking and kissing a trail along her jawline and down to her earlobe with his talented lips and tongue. He drew the tender lobe into his mouth and lightly nibbled. Rain's breath hitched as bursts of sensual delight showered over her before centering in the area of her clit. Releasing a low moan of need, she lifted her hips in eager anticipation of the next penetration.

"Shit, this is good. So good," Jet bit out. "Fuck our mate, Garrett, just like I'm fucking you."

Garrett grunted and trembled, his respirations increasing, along with the length of his thrusts.

Rain writhed under Garrett's large body, pressing closer, needing everything he could give and then some. Her arousal escalated to a fevered pitch, leaving her desperate for release, a bliss she simply couldn't reach. A whimper escaped as she struggled to latch onto the elusive catalyst to send her spiraling in delicious free fall.

"So close." Garrett lapped at her nipple, bringing the tip to taut attention.

Only the sound of a moan or whimper broke through the harmony of their slapping bodies and combined struggle to suck in air.

Heat blanketed her like a hot bath. Her body demanded extra, making her squirm and whine, dig her nails into Garrett's back, and clamor for more.

"Damn. Her scent is driving me nuts."

"I think her heat's peaking," Garrett tossed out as he changed from one breast to the other.

"Why do you say that?" Jet asked.

"Because she's dancing on my dick like there's no tomorrow." Garrett growled as he drew her nipple into his mouth.

Her heat provided the base, their individual scents joined in, combining into an unmistakably alluring and intoxicating aroma which permeated the room—the scent of their mating and matehood. She recognized the difference absently, but was too distracted to think much of it. All she knew is that with every inhalation, her lust jacked up another large step.

Rain heard the conversation but couldn't focus enough to participate. Her entire attention remained on Garrett delivering erotic pleasure to her needy body. He rammed in harder, delving to maximum depths on every powerful stroke. His teeth lightly nipping her nipple drove her nearly mad with arousal. Still, she couldn't find the key to unlocking the most glorious climax of her life.

Frantically, she wiggled, locking her legs around Garrett's back in an effort to pull him into her body, to merge them as one unity, to finally get him to strum her throbbing clit in an effort to relieve the tension racking her body.

"Shit." Garrett braced himself above her, his eyes narrowing to slits. He tilted his head back and arched his back.

The action rubbed a tender area. She leaped a step closer. With an inarticulate cry, she braced herself for the upcoming maelstrom.

"Rain. Just let go." Jet's voice carried to her ears.

She shook her head against the pillow. If she'd had any rational thought left, she would've been a bit afraid of the massively growing rapture within her loins. Instead, she fought and clawed, anything to get to that point. "I can't. It's too much." With such a build-up of fiery passion she knew she would shatter to pieces in the resulting explosion. Yet, none of that mattered — nothing except reaching the peak.

Finding Garrett's shoulder right in front of her eyes, she opened wide and sank her teeth in.

"Fuck." Garrett surged into her once more, his knot beginning to swell. He pinned her with his gaze. "I've got you, Rain. Trust me. I won't let anything happen to you. Just trust me and come."

"Damn it, Rain. Just. Let. Go." The commanding tone from Jet nudged her to the very brink.

Garrett humped once more, shoving the nearly full gland into her channel then locking in place.

She arched her lower back, felt the bump against her cervix, then silently screamed as powerful contractions rippled through her body, each one tightly squeezing her channel on Garrett's buried dick, only adding to the brilliant orgasm. Her world spun with the near violent crests, leaving her to hold on with her teeth, arms, and legs, in a futile effort to maintain her sanity through the unending waves. Blackness threatened until she managed to inhale then receded, taking her strength with it.

After releasing her bite, Rain crumpled back against the bed, completely drained from one of the most intense, yet satisfying, experiences of her life.

Garrett flattened out over her body, his weight welcome where she needed closeness more than anything else. Glancing up, she found Jet still kneeling behind Garrett, his expression of either agony or unrivaled ecstasy. She'd have bet on the latter.

She struggled to catch her breath, still tied to Garrett in the most elemental way possible. He groaned now and again, rocking slightly with Jet still topping him and buried deep. Their faces scrunched and hips jerked now and again, in obvious rapture as their climaxes continued on and on. She easily felt Garrett's still bulging knot holding them together and knew Jet's cock would be the same way. Not about to complain, she savored the moment, resting up for the next round sure to come right on the heels of the last.

*At least this is a sterile heat.* She grinned to herself, enjoying the idiosyncrasies of nature when it came to shifters. This heat might mark true mates but pregnancy wouldn't occur. Like the lions of the wild, when a new male took over the pride, the females went into immediate heat, yet none would breed. Nature's way of ensuring stability existed before cubs became a concern. It was the same way with shifters. She'd gladly step into motherhood. Later. Much later. After all, she had centuries left before her ability to conceive declined.

Filled to the brink, Rain knew she'd only be content for a moment. She studied the two men who had been thrown into her path, stepped up to the plate, and moved heaven and earth for her.

*A woman could do worse. Much worse.* Than spend the next nine hundred plus years with her true mates. Men with big hearts, generosity, and bravery. Two alphas who came together as one.

Several days ago, Rain had thought her life had ended with an order to find a mate or suffer the one appointed for her. Now, she realized that, while a rough way to go, fate had forced her to open herself to love.

As long as she lived, she'd soar with Jet and Garrett, sharing her life with the men she loved more than her own life.

"Damn. I can't stop." Garrett's knot had disappeared, allowing him to move inside her eager channel once more. His eyes met hers in wicked playfulness.

"Enjoy it, baby." Jet's low voice carried in a whisper. "I have a feeling it's always going to be like this between us."

"I hope that's the case," she blurted on a yip as passion resurged.

Garrett chuckled. "No worries. I think, between the three of us, we can manage."

They did just that. More than managed. Set the sheets on fire, fulfilled each one of her fantasies, and finally crumpled into a heap, too tired to do more than hold one another.

She didn't need experience to know she'd found loving perfection. Her two men showed her—over and over again.

# Chapter Eighteen

Garrett slid off the bed, careful to avoid jarring the other two occupants, still asleep after a morning full of carnal activities—hot, wonderful, orgasmic carnal activities. Standing, he gazed down at his two mates and couldn't help but grin. Jet and Rain still snuggled together, his arm wrapped protectively around her. Garrett had found himself in the same position on her opposite side until a few minutes before. Evidently, even in their sleep, both he and Jet made sure to take care of their newest mate.

His stomach growled with hunger. With a rueful shake of his head, he grabbed a pair of loose sweats from the dresser before heading out of the bedroom, quiet steps which took him first to the bathroom, then to the kitchen. At the moment, he could've eaten a wildebeest and was pretty sure his mates would face the same problem when they awoke.

*Looks like I'm the cook this morning.* Absently, he noted the clock. *Make that early afternoon.*

He didn't mind. Always before, he and Jet had shared the cooking duties, although neither claimed to be a proficient chef. Instead, they relied on the basics and went out to eat now and again when a craving for something fancier hit. Breakfast, luckily, fell under the easy category and he could navigate through that particular meal easily.

As he gathered food from the refrigerator, his thoughts turned back to last night and this morning. Rain's heat had hit hard and fast, not only signifying their status as true mates, but challenging him and Jet to keep up with her endless horniness. He'd only dreamed about such events in the past and the reality far bypassed his greatest expectations.

He bent over to get a skillet from the cabinet and felt the rawness of his cock rubbing against the soft cotton material. The slight sting told him his manhood had been hard used, perhaps over used. Obviously, there were a few consequences for hours of non-stop sex during mating heat. While tender, he wasn't about to utter a single complaint. He'd gladly trade in some minor chafing for another marathon bout of some of the best sex ever.

His mind still reeled from all that had happened in so short a time. Discovering Rain and dealing with Jet's insistence at a mating to someone he'd met a minute before. The deaths. The blame he'd placed on Rain's innocent shoulders.

He cringed at the way he'd treated her and vowed once more to make everything up to her. After all, they had a lifetime and he had more than enough penance to perform.

Then the betrayal by the only father he truly remembered and the resulting battle. For a split second he'd considered returning to his original pack, but had quickly dismissed the idea while lying in the healer's bed impatiently waiting for permission to return home.

Home. In Spring Hill Pack with Jet and Rain. For as long as they lived.

The thought brought him peace and comfort. Not everyone had his good fortune and he wasn't about to screw up the best things in his life.

By the time he dropped the last slice of sausage into the already heated skillet, Jet ambled into the room, his black hair tousled, and wearing only a pair of jeans, the rest of him bare.

Garrett raked Jet with his gaze and grinned saucily. "You look a little worse for wear." Jet appeared as appealing as ever with scruffy two day old whiskers and sleepiness in his normally bright, flashing eyes. "Like you just dragged yourself over the finish line of a triathlon."

Jet rolled his eyes. "More like an insatiable mate in heat. Both of you."

Garrett snorted. "Hey, I was more than ready to raise the white flag about three hours ago, but someone kept licking my cock then hammering my ass."

A sly grin appeared on Jet's face. "Oh, yeah."

"Uh huh." Garrett shook his head and turned the burner down on the boiling eggs.

Jet opened the cupboard and pulled out a mug. "Are you as sore as I am?"

"Probably more so, but it was damn worth it."

"Oh, yeah." Jet poured his coffee and took a sip. "Up for another round soon?"

Garrett groaned at the thought. His normally eager cock didn't even stir at the subtle hint. Totally worn out, he needed some time to recover — more like days. But, deep down he knew if Rain walked in and shot him a pleading look, he'd return to bed and pleasure her until she asked him to stop, no matter anything else. Jet was on his own. He chuckled to himself. Odd how that thought ran through his mind. Before Rain appeared, he'd decided Jet was all he needed. Now, he'd give her the world if he could. "I now know why females search out a couple of men to satisfy them during their heat. Hell, one man just wouldn't be up to the task, no matter how hard they tried."

"If he did, he's a damn sight better than me."

Jet set the table for three places then dropped bread in the toaster while Garrett flipped the sausage. "Think we should wake Rain?"

Garrett considered the notion for a moment. "Nah. Poor thing has to be worn completely out. If we're sore and tired imagine how such a small woman like her must feel."

"Good point. We'll leave leftovers if the smell of breakfast doesn't wake her."

After taking up the ready food, Garrett headed to the table. Jet lowered to the chair first, in his usual spot, as Garrett placed the platter of meat and eggs in easy reach. Taking his chair, Garrett watched Jet fill his plate and dig in hungrily. He could empathize.

They had taken only a few bites when Rain appeared wearing Jet's discarded shirt, the tails hanging to mid-thigh while the top sagged low enough to hint at her modest cleavage. Her long hair glistened in the afternoon light, appearing freshly brushed and bound by a ribbon. "This smells delicious."

Jet pulled a chair out and patted it. "Join us."

Gracefully, Rain navigated the distance, her steps gliding, not the least bit hesitant or jerky. She sat down somewhat gingerly then wiggled in her seat.

Garrett met Jet's gaze, sharing a knowing look. Rain was just as tender as they were. He studied her closely, finding fatigue and weariness on her face, though her eyes remained as sharp and clear as always. Sniffing, he detected only a hint of what had radiated from her hours before. The fact proved significant in meaning. Rain's heat had peaked and had now faded quickly. He would have been disappointed if not for their bodies' need for a reprieve to recover from such an erotically superb, yet exhausting, experience.

"How are you feeling?" Jet posed the question on Garrett's mind.

She shrugged and began filling her plate. "Tired but fine."

"Not desperate for our cocks?" Jet grinned rakishly.

"Ummm. No. I think that part is just about done." Rain rolled her eyes before winking at Garrett.

"That's too bad. I had all these fantasies to try today."

Garrett chuckled and leaned over to whisper to Rain loud enough for their third mate to hear. "You'll have to forgive him. He's a sex addict. Has been since I've known him."

"Somehow that doesn't surprise me in the least." She snorted then ruined the effect with a giggle.

He paused for a moment. "But, what he's not admitting is you kicked his butt. Completely."

Rain arched an eyebrow directed at Jet. "Did little old me wear the big bad alpha out?"

Jet narrowed his eyes for a brief moment before he shook his head with a wicked grin. "Fine. I'll confess. You kicked both our asses."

"And they say women are the weaker sex." Rain lifted her chin haughtily.

"Not touching that with a broom handle." Jet speared a piece of sausage and took a bite.

"Don't worry. We love you, both in and out of bed," Garrett added with a bright smile. He found the bantering fun and relaxing, a tribute to the bond they'd discovered over the past few days.

"What are we going to do today?" Rain sank her teeth into a piece of toast slathered with butter and jelly.

"Whatever you want. I'm still on light duty and house arrest." Garrett shot Jet a look of annoyance.

Jet didn't even flinch. "Hey, I came too close to losing you to rush your recovery."

"Yeah, well, I'd say I'm fully recovered considering all the exercise I got the past twenty-four hours." Garrett took a large bite of egg.

"True." Jet grinned and sipped his coffee. "Just call me selfish then."

Rain took a bite of sausage and gazed up at both men, a serious expression on her face.

Taking the hint, Garrett peered down at her. "Is there something you need to do?"

She finished chewing and nodded. "I need to call my associate at the shop and give her the deal of a lifetime."

Garrett glanced over at Jet, reading the anticipation in Jet's black eyes. Steeling himself, he asked the burning question. "The deal of a lifetime?"

"Yep. I'm going to offer to let her buy the store at a more than fair market value and take over the lease on the shop and the apartment above it." She met Garrett's gaze, then reached out her hand.

He didn't hesitate to wrap her fingers in his, noting Jet did the same on the other side.

"I know everything happened so fast, but I made a decision this morning. No way do I want to return to my previous life amongst the humans. I love you both and need to be with you, not an hour down the road pining away for my mates."

"Are you sure?" Jet asked quietly.

"Positive."

"We wouldn't ask that of you." Garrett bit back his excitement and relief, needing for her to be absolutely certain. He, for one, wasn't about to give her up. Yet, he couldn't ask her to give up everything she'd worked so hard for in order to be with them.

She beamed up at him. "You don't have to. I'm more than willing." She hesitated a second then continued. "You see...I can't live without a heart and you both have mine."

Garrett kissed her hand, unable to quell the brilliant grin. Jet did the same, appearing more than thrilled with her words.

After a rough start with Rain, he sat beside her at the breakfast table, nearly bursting with emotion with her sweet confession for him and Jet alike.

"I'm the luckiest shifter alive." Jet arched an eyebrow. "With the two finest mates around."

"Yeah, I didn't do too badly either. Although dealing with an alpha with a stick up his butt gives me gray hair."

"Takes one to know one."

Rain burst out laughing.

Garrett found the sound music to his ears. Yeah, he thought his life perfect before and had been too stiff and unbending to give Rain a chance. Now, he exalted in not only having their perfect third and a true mating to boot, but he could also now feel free to express exactly who he was.

An alpha with an all-consuming love for his mates.

# Epilogue

*One month later*

"I'm going to miss you." Autumn finished emptying the cash register for the day, stuffed the money into a bank bag, and zipped the top.

"I'll come back and visit. You can't get rid of me that easily." Rain smiled at her friend and former employee. She'd decided to offer her business to Autumn, give her a discount if she wanted to purchase the fabric store for herself. She wouldn't have minded staying on as sole owner if Autumn wouldn't have got the loan, as long as her best friend took over the store. Luckily, the bank hadn't batted an eyelid and had offered her a low interest loan, making the payments affordable, especially if Autumn moved into apartment above the store, just as Rain had done before.

"You'd better. Besides, I might need help now and again."

Rain waved her hand. "You've been running this business more than I have for the past year. I know you can handle it. However, you've got my phone number. Call anytime."

"Don't think I won't," Autumn threatened with mock sternness, then followed with a hug. "Promise to keep in touch."

"Promise."

The cheerful ring of the front door bell announced visitors. Rain glanced up.

Autumn whistled softly. "No wonder you sold out. I would too if I could play with them full time."

"Yeah, when it had come down to an actual decision about living an hour away to run the fabric store or moving in with them, it was a no-brainer." Rain smiled as she watched the two men in her life enter the store and walk down the center aisle. Both nearly glowed with handsomeness. Jet wore black jeans with a long-sleeved black T-shirt. His penchant for black amused her these days. Garrett chose a softer color, going for blue jeans and a tan-colored shirt that brought out the color of his eyes. Strong, fit, and vibrant with health, they both took her breath away.

Her friend chuckled. "Definitely. Now if they only had a brother or three I could date." With a forlorn sigh, she walked toward the back office, the day's money in hand.

"Hi." Jet stopped right in front of the main counter.

"Hi, yourself." Rain leaned across the wooden barrier to meet Garrett's kiss of greeting.

"Hey now. None of that. We've got to get a move on, or we'll be late to the celebration." Jet nudged Garrett aside and pressed his lips to Rain's.

Rain chuckled, recognizing Jet's attempt to use the big event as an excuse to pry Garrett from her so Jet could take his place for the moment. They had plenty of time to return home, get cleaned up, then head to the celebration.

As a silver lining to the recent fiasco, Horizon and Spring Hill had made the combined decision to forget the past and start anew. Their mating appeared to bond more than the three of them. Today, both packs were pulled together to watch as the alphas signed a treaty for the ages, promising peace and friendship between the two groups. Golden Branch had been invited, but as they were still hammering out the issue of who would take the supreme alpha seat, they declined—for now. Hope still existed that once the smaller group stabilized, they would come forth and join the alliance.

The animosity between them might not immediately dissipate. However, this had to be considered a major step in the right direction.

"So?" she teased.

"So, I just got your father to halfway like me. Let's not make him reconsider such generosity."

"Good thing he's liked me all along. I don't have to live up to such standards." Garrett winked at Rain.

"Uh huh." Jet elbowed him in the ribs.

Rain giggled at their antics. After grabbing her purse, she pulled the strap over her shoulder, rounded the counter, and followed them to the front door. There she paused, turned, and stared at the basis of her life for the past few years.

"Regrets?" Jet asked quietly.

She shook her head. "I might miss the place, but it's not where I need to be."

Garrett twined his fingers with hers. Jet did the same on the opposite side. Her gaze flicked from one to the other. "I belong where my mates are."

"Even if it means living in the middle of a desert?" Jet asked.

"Or right next door to the ruling alpha?" Garrett smiled and lifted her hand for a brush of his lips.

She shuddered dramatically then broke the playacting by laughing. "Even if I had to live at the North Pole. I'd go anywhere you two wanted. After all, you both have my heart."

They smiled widely, expressions of love, pride, and tenderness covered each of their faces. She beamed in return, so very pleased with her mates.

"Then let's go home." Jet led the way.

Just where Rain wanted to be. Home with her loving mates. Sharing their lives for the centuries to come. She couldn't imagine anything in the world could make her happier than Jet and Garrett. Her dream had come true, though in an amazing roundabout way.

They stepped out into the sunshine and into the next stage of their very long lives. Together.

# About the Author

Growing up in the Midwest, I began reading romance novels in high school, immediately falling in love with the genre, to the point where I decided to write professionally for a career. However, that dream splattered against a brick wall, resulting in a quick death in my first writing class in college when my professor told me bluntly that I wasn't any good at it. I shifted gears quickly, and left my writing dreams behind, eventually settling on becoming a nurse.

A few years back, I stumbled across a fan-fiction writing site on a favorite author's webpage. I began to read stories others wrote, not only making some wonderful close friends from the experience, but also, really learning to write for the very first time. Here I was able to share short stories, practice my writing skills, and truly develop into a writer. More than that, the experience allowed me to revitalize my dream, as I rediscovered joy in writing. Now, I spend my days off with my alpha male characters, quick witted heroines, and see how much trouble everyone can get into.

When I'm not working or writing, I enjoy working in the garden, canning, and seeing my backyard as a living canvas for my whimsical landscaping, and, of course, reading romance novels.

Cheyenne Meadows loves to hear from readers. You can find her contact information, website details and author profile page at http://www.totallybound.com.

Totally Bound Publishing

5 MAGN 00035190 4

CPSIA information can be obtained at www.ICGtesting.com
Printed in the USA
LVOW12s1434270115

424563LV00001B/93/P

9 781784 303075